Margot
Margaret
Marjorie
Margarida

like so many pearls
before a swine

a love story

Warren Laine-Naida

Margarethe
Margriet
Margista
Marjatta

This book is dedicated to every poor swine who has followed in the footsteps of the woman he loved in the hope that she will drop a pearl.

"Do not give dogs what is sacred; do not throw your pearls to pigs. If you do, they may trample them under their feet, and turn and tear you to pieces."

Matthew 7:6

the dangers of pearl diving, pig farming, and falling in love

Your garden variety love stories begin with a kiss, a stolen glance, or a meeting in Paris or Venice, and often it's by chance. Most love stories need suffering, too, at least at the end. Tragic accidents fill the pages of love stories. So, while these stories are about everyday love, it seems appropriate to bring in some element of danger, at least to make us thankful that every character leaves the pages as you find them. Uninjured but in love.

From pointed sticks in muddy fields to poisonous jellyfish lurking in tranquil seaside pools, no good story about pearls or our porcine friends in front of which we scatter them would be complete without a dangerous moment or two.

Before we can cast the first pearl in front of our swine, they need to be harvested, which is mostly now done artificially. In the early days, divers had to swim into the depths to find the oysters harbouring the treasures. Gritty work indeed. It's an almost obsolete trade now, but some still hunt for pearls recreationally. Pearl diving can be dangerous. Even fatal.

The downside to collecting pearls for your sweetheart is manifold. Drowning, of course, is at the top of the list of dangers. You need to dive deep for an oyster. Decompression sickness is another, especially if you return to the surface too quickly.

The cold water thirty to forty feet down means you run the risk of hypothermia, too, possibly leading to a heart attack. If you survive all that, you may run into a jellyfish or other venomous creature. You could also bang your head against a rock or cut yourself quite nastily trying to swim away from danger.

Raising a cute pig on a farm must be an idyllic life compared to pearl diving. However, all that oinks is not gold. If you work with swine, you also run the risk of injury and illness.

On the pig farm, you could stick yourself with one of the many needles used for vaccines. Your wound may become contaminated by animal waste. You may even have an allergic reaction. Infections can also be transmitted between swine and people. Swine influenza, scabies, ringworm, toxoplasmosis, salmonellosis, and trichinosis come to mind.

In addition, there are countless farm injuries like being hit by equipment to add to our list of dangers. There are chains, sprockets, and pulleys that can lacerate and crush us as we go about our work. And don't forget the smell. You're going to need a mask and probably a self-contained source of air if you spend too much time in the pigsty.

The cool, crisp, tropical waters of the lagoon seem positively inviting now. I think I might take my chances with the jellyfish.

Compared to a nasty jellyfish sting or losing a finger in a hog snare, there is no visible damage after you have fallen in love. You fall, you get up, you move on. Maybe you walk a bit like a drunkard for a time. That might be an advantage because it will keep people away. You will have time to heal. There may be some aching. Recovery is often swift, but there can be an extended period of lingering trauma.

Compared with the dangers of pearl diving and pig farming, falling in love is a walk in the park. I've fallen in love so many times I have the equivalent of broken bones but not yet any serious internal injuries.

Ego is the first victim in the triage of love. A bruised ego is a terrible patient. Lungs, heart, liver, sexual organs – all get a good workout, but if you are lucky, they are not much worse for wear at the end of each bout. Secondary victims at best. Tertiary victims are the aptly named bystanders, friends, and family.

Falling in love. It's a bit like the flu, or Covid, which felt much like the flu to me. Have you succumbed? Have you survived the fall? I followed all the precautions. Social distancing, immunization, I wore protection even when others did not. I religiously kept myself clean and topped up with vitamins and other preventatives, both homeopathic and industrially concocted. I still got battered and bruised. I toed the line, and I still fell in love. Oh, I got Covid too.

After a while falling in love becomes much like any other addiction. You need to hit yourself harder the next time to feel anything. That sounds harsh. It's not meant to. Let me rephrase that.

You go in for another round because it felt so good the previous times. That bruising. You need to hit yourself harder to get through the scarred epidermal layer. Here I don't mean that protective layer between the elements and what's beneath our skin. Deeper even than our heart. It's our ego that protects us from the harsher elements to be found out there.

Our heart needs protection from physical and ethereal elements, but very little protection is available. There's no umbrella, gloves, or even lip balm to protect our hearts. If there were, I guess they couldn't protect well enough against all those arrows. All those barbs. We don't stand a chance.

Pleasure can be imagined, but pain is very real and probably the best reminder that we are alive. The shortness. The fear. The finger tremulously held a fraction of an inch above the bubbles of hot sugar as it boils and pops in the pot. The knife gingerly removing the still-warm toast. The kiss we make with our eyes closed and during which anything could happen.

When we fall in love, we open ourselves to the frightening tenuousness of it all.

Like So Many Pearls Before a Swine: A Love Story

Margot
Margaret
Marjorie
Margarida

part one two three

Margarethe
Margriet
Margisia
Marjolein

margot

Any thoughts of injuries sustained in the water or on the farm are far from either of our minds as Margot and I speed through the sun-drenched Alsace countryside. The rented sports car is insistent that I drive with both hands. Margot, vibrant in a summer dress of pink coral, is tightly seat-belted. The only pain either of us feels is our impatience.

Possibly it is the pain of my hangover. I'm a polite but very resolute wine taster. It may also be our desire. We are nearing the end of a frustrating three-hour drive between hotels where, upon arrival in Equisheim, an hour of pleasure may await us.

Strands of Margot's soft black hair, not held in place by the scarf on her head, fly out behind her. She turns to smile at me, overjoyed by the week away from papers and patients. The sun reflects off her large, black sunglasses, so I cannot see her eyes, but I know they're smiling too.

She turns back to her open window, drinking in the vineyards and the stork-filled rooftops, waving her hand gently against the wind as we pass the Eguisheim exit.

"Oh!" Margot turns to me, her red lips forming an O that exposes the tiny pearls of her teeth.

I nod and slow down, pulling over to the side of the road, preparing to U-turn. "Sorry. You distracted me." I look over to her, wink, and turn my attention back to the mirrors, waiting for my chance to cross the road.

"I never said a word."

"You smiled."

She reaches over and squeezes my hand with her soft, warm fingers, then turns to look out the back window.

"I'm thirsty. Will we be there in time?"

"Plenty of time." I lie. "There's a bottle of water in the glove compartment." I nod. "I'm parched as well."

Each time you fall, the bruising, while invisible, thickens your skin, but I only ever lie to Margot about little things. I could never wantonly lie to her. Close your eyes and say her name. Gently. Margot. Now try other variations. Margareta. Margrit. Malgosia. It's like invoking the name of a saint.

So, I lie about the peripherals without any pangs of conscience. The price of a jar of ginger marmalade, the price of a restaurant meal, or in this case, the starting time of a small French provincial wine festival.

"I'm sorry about your headache. You know you're not supposed to swallow the wine when you taste it." She laughs, squeezes my hand again, and removes her sunglasses. "I can hold out if you want to drink the water."

I shake my head. "I'll be fine."

In between mirror checks, I turn and smile at Margot. I admire in bite-sized glances her hair as it curls about her ears, the fine lines around her almond-shaped eyes, the fullness of her red lips, and the curve of her neck as she stretches to look out the window.

This is the third time I've fallen in love with Margot. Or possibly the fourth. Maybe I have always been in love with her, and each time is simply a new iteration, like a software update. I never said I was a romantic; I said I very often fell in love.

I've tried to lie about loving her, but it never really sticks. Not even I believed it. Margot has believed me from time to time, causing me further bruising. Honestly, though, if you can't lie to yourself, then you've probably no real vocation for deceit.

"Clear!" Margot calls and turns back in her seat. She presses the seatbelt back into place and sits back, brushing the hair from her eyes and replacing her sunglasses.

I turn the car into the road, accelerate, and drive the hundred or so metres back to the exit we had just passed.

Eguisheim is a lovely town in the middle of the Alsace countryside. It's small and easily overlooked, being off the main tourist route running between Strasbourg and Colmar, but worth the extra few kilometres drive.

The town has never had more than about fifteen hundred residents, even though it's existed since Roman times. It's the birthplace of Pope Leo the ninth. Or is it the eleventh? Back in the eleventh century, at any rate. We're there for the wine, not the history – if the two can be separated. The town has quite a few wineries, of which my favourite is only about three hundred years old. Domaine Freudenreich Joseph. Honestly, I was first attracted to their wine labels, but I fell in love with their wine over the years.

Our hotel is small, but it's on the main street and within walking distance of the centre of town, which after a wine tasting, is probably a good consideration.

"Bonjour. Nous avons réservé une chambre. Le nom est Beech."

The secret to getting a good room at a French hotel is to let your French-speaking girlfriend check you in.

We can hear music coming from the centre of town, and small crowds of people make their way back and forth, some returning with wine glasses and bottles in their hands, others going towards the centre with empty hands. The wine festival has obviously already begun.

"It's a bit odd that none of the wineries here is much older than the seventeen hundreds." Margot walks along the cobblestone streets, taking photos with her SLR camera. She likes to develop her shots into black and white prints. They're really quite beautiful. "The town's so old. I'd expected something from; I don't know. Much older, anyway. Thirteen, fourteen hundred."

"There's Dopff. It's in Riquewihr, back towards Strasbourg. We can drive there the day after tomorrow if you like. They're the oldest in Alsace, I think. Fifteen hundred something. The oldest one in France began in the eleventh century actually. I can't remember the name. It's still in operation."

"Where is it?"

"Hmm, don't remember that either." I purse my lips. "I could Google it."

"No. That's fine." Margot leans against the fountain. "Take a photo of me?"

She passes me her camera. "I'm always afraid I'll drop it."

Margot laughs. "Your phone cost more than my camera. You never think twice about dropping that."

"We're all so immune to tech." I hold up the camera and peer into the viewfinder. "It's our disposable society." I hand her camera back.

"Thank you." She takes the camera and reaches for my hand. "Let's walk a bit before going to the wine festival?"

"Yes. Good idea. All that sitting. Are you sure I can't tempt you back to the hotel for some … ?"

Margot laughs, shaking her head. "Uh-uh. Later."

"Your camera is like a museum piece. I've lost connection to things like that. I'm terrified of breaking it."

Margot laughs. "You're funny."

"I'm glad you think so. I doubt any of my insurance covers breaking your camera."

She moves closer and presses her head against my shoulder. "Don't worry. I have it insured."

"Well, make sure I'm careful with it."

"Of course." She turns her face to me, and we pause, exchanging a kiss and stopping longer than necessary to enjoy it. "It's a beautiful afternoon."

"You're the beautiful afternoon."

She blushes, and we renew our slow pace up the street, finally reaching the wall that rings the medieval town.

"Left or right?" I ask.

Margot looks both ways, sizing them up in her viewfinder. "Left."

We move in that direction. "Why?"

"The light is better there. And there's an interesting door. Do you see it?"

"You always notice these sorts of things."

"Do I?"

"It's one of the many reasons I like you."

"Quantify 'many'."

"Oh, I don't know. More than one less than twenty?"

"You have less than twenty reasons you like me?"

"Umm, well, when I say 'like', I'm differentiating between those reasons I like you and those reasons I adore you."

"I'm interested in seeing your list when you have time." Margot laughs, stopping to take a photo of an ancient-looking window recessed into the sloping wall of an impossibly built house. "They couldn't have built it like this."

"It's probably settled over the last thousand years. I can't imagine there were steel girders or concrete supports when this was built."

"Wattle and daub."

"Excuse me?"

"Didn't they build with wattle and daub?"

"I've no idea. I would have thought timber and … well timber and whatever the material in between might be." I reach out and run my hand over the plaster.

"That's wattle and daub. I read that wattle and daub buildings can last more than five hundred years in the right climate."

"Fascinating."

"You never answered my question."

"About building materials, or the other thing?"

"Why you adore me."

"Ah! A lot of reasons. Wait for my list."

"Coward."

"Not cowardly. Judicious."

Margot rolls her eyes. "We might need to go back."

The lane ends at a high wall on three sides. We look around, but there is no way to go left or right.

"You're right."

Margot turns her camera up and photographs the ramparts running above us. "This is where they would have poured the boiling oil and water on us."

"Excuse me?"

"We'd have been trapped. No way out but back. There would have been soldiers blocking the way we came. At the very least armed peasants."

"Your imagination."

"It's not my imagination. I bet that's why this was built in this way."

"It's one of the things I adore about you. Your imagination."

Margot purses her lips. "Hmm. Well, I still want to see your list."

"Let's hope we get out of this alive, then."

She laughs, and we walk towards the town centre.

margaret

I look up from the large desk we share as Margaret pads in barefoot from the kitchen across the threadbare carpet. She smiles at me and places her tea down on the stained, wooden desktop. Then she sits down and resumes work, looking over the rims of her glasses as she reads whatever is on the screen of her laptop.

"I can't work with you staring at me."

I turn my attention back to the latest article, which is not yet late for submission but bordering on being on time. I pride myself on submitting everything a few days before the deadline.

"I was hardly *staring*." I look up, seeing the top of her head as she moves in closer to her screen to verify a footnote or similar textual tidbit.

Margaret's fingers tap at her keyboard for a moment, then find the staccato rhythm I recognize as being the introduction to something. She does not look up.

"You were intently looking."

"I like looking at you."

"Call it a fixation."

"Call it adoration."

Margaret's keyboard goes silent.

"You know I don't like that word. The connotation is that you have me on a pedestal. I could fall. You could push me." Her keyboard starts up again.

"I would never do that."

"You could stop adoring me and leave me on the pedestal to starve." She stops typing and looks up at me. "You've done it before."

"Not intentionally." I look down and hit the keys of my keyboard with uncertainty. "You never starved."

"I was for long periods very hungry." There is a pause. "And sad."

"I know." I close my eyes, typing erratically. I open my eyes and look at the screen, wondering what Etymologists would make of the word 'msicepay'. "I'm sorry."

The room fills with the sounds of hurried prose mixed with our silence. Ideas quickly but lightly made into words that fill our screens which will later, after the whiny zip of our laserjet printer, appear on paper.

"Adoration. Loving admiration and devotion. To be fond of." I lunge.

"Like fond of apple pie? Or a cocker spaniel?" She parries.

"I'm here." My riposte sounds weak.

"Imagine my gratitude." Her counterattack was unexpected, but I'm still on my feet.

"No." I feint. "I'm here because I don't want to be anywhere else. I'm here because I love you." I raise myself slightly in my chair, looking over her laptop and into her eyes, which raise to meet mine.

"I know." She smiles, her mouth and her eyes working in harmony to produce a beatific glow of pleasure. "I'm teasing you."

"Oh." I sit down again. "Alright." I reach over for my coffee cup and drink the last of the now cold liquid. "I really am sorry, though. For before. I'll always be sorry for making you unhappy."

Her hand reaches out between the stacks of books that define her side of the desk from mine and takes up her teacup. The cup moves out of my line of sight, and I hear her gentle slurps.

"I know." There are further cat-like slurps. "I love you too."

I sit back, look at the article and my empty coffee cup, and then stand up and move towards the kitchen. Margaret reaches out and takes my hand as I pass.

"Bring me a cookie?"

I nod and smile.

The drip coffee maker sitting on the kitchen counter is not of my choosing. When I moved in, I made a pact to live on someone else's terms instead of my own for a change. My own terms hadn't done me much good in retrospect, so perhaps Margaret's would serve me better.

I rinse the glass container, refill it with cold water, and fill the machine. Then I take out a coffee filter, fit it into the basket, and scoop seven spoons of dark ground coffee into the filter. When that is done, I turn on the machine and lean against the counter to wait. Then I remember Margaret's cookie.

I take out two Hobnobs from the crinkly, orange plastic package sitting on the counter, place these on a small plate, and take them into the other room. When I return, the coffee machine is emitting its first steam-laden grunts.

After a few minutes, the coffee belches from its innards; I stand there looking out the small kitchen window and wait with great anticipation. Annie pads in, tail wagging and panting gently.

"Hey there." I reach down and stroke her head. "Thirsty?"

I reach down for her empty water dish, refill it, then replace the red plastic bowl on the floor. Annie begins eagerly lapping at the cool water as Margaret walks into the kitchen.

"Would you mind taking Annie for a walk? I don't want to lose my concentration on this piece."

"Sure. I'm stuck anyway."

"I'm sure you're not stuck. You're just distracted."

"Fencing with you? Possibly." I walk over to the kitchen door and remove Annie's leash. "Maybe I'm just horny seeing you in that thin summer dress."

Margaret snorts, gently smacking my hand away as I reach for her. "Your being in a constant state of arousal would be different how?"

I laugh. "I just put my foil away. I can't do another bout with you." I kiss her forehead. "Come on, Annie. Shall we go out for a walk?"

"What about your coffee?"

"I'll get one while we're out."

Margaret nods. "It's hot out. Keep to the shade if you can."

"We'll go to the park."

"Thank you."

I smile, and Annie walks eagerly into the hallway, excitedly wagging her tail and pressing against my legs.

"Shall I bring anything back?"

Margaret leans against the wall, crossing her arms closing her eyes. Her skin is covered in a thin layer of glistening sweat. "Hmm. I can't think of anything."

She pushes herself away from the wall and walks into the kitchen. I hear the refrigerator door opening and, after a few seconds closing again. I hear her rummaging through the fruit bowl next to it. Margaret comes back out into the hallway and raises her eyebrows. "Lemons?"

"Lemons."

She nods. "Please. And if they have any persimmons, perhaps two or three?"

I look down at Annie. "Hear that? We're going to the market. Maybe you'll get some sausage."

Margaret closes her eyes and exhales. "Only a small bit, please. The vet says she's getting too much salt."

"Okay." I nod and open the door. Annie runs out, and I follow, turning to Margaret. "See you later then."

Margaret has followed us to the door, which she holds ajar. "Bye, Annie. Be a good girl."

Annie barks excitedly, and we take the stairs to the ground floor two at a time. I stop at the front door to attach her leash, and then the two of us walk out into the bright sunshine of the street.

marjorie

The train is thankfully only half full. There is no way to reserve a seat on the regional city service, which is normally full at this time of the morning. Happily, other factors have kept people at home, so the seats across the aisle from us and those in front are free of passengers.

She smiles. "It's nice."

I place my coffee cup on the small metal table cum windowsill before I remove my jacket. "It is. Can I put your jacket up top?"

Marjorie nods. "Please." I fold mine in half, place it on the rack above our heads, then take hers and gently lay it on top of mine.

She laughs. "It's not silk."

"Hmm?" I sit down and gratefully take my coffee and sip. "What isn't silk?"

"My jacket." Marjorie places her hand on my arm and squeezes gently. "It's okay if it gets dirty."

I laugh. "Sorry. I know." I lean over, and we kiss. I move my head back and look at her face, letting my eyes linger over hers, feeling very happy to be taking this trip together. "I'm trying my best to be gallant."

"You're very kind."

"You're very special."

The train jerks suddenly, and I hold onto my coffee cup.

"Looks like we're off." I look out the window as the platform retreats away from us. I turn back to Marjorie. "Looking forward to the day?"

"Oh yes. It will be nice to do some shopping. And I'm looking forward to lunch. It's a treat."

"It's been too long." I nod, agreeing.

We both lean back in our chairs and smile, glad to be breaking the pattern of work and home the last few months have ingrained upon us.

She turns to me, and I turn back from the window. "Thank you again for the flowers. They're beautiful."

I laugh and roll my eyes. "Oh! You're welcome. How embarrassing. I'm sorry. I ordered them to be delivered yesterday. When you didn't say anything, I couldn't think of a way to query. The florists were no help at all."

Marjorie laughs, deep and sensual. Sensual is a term I always come back to when I think of her. Sexy seems too girlish for Marjorie. Sensual. Deeply sensual.

"It worked out fine. I was just walking out the door. Lucky they arrived when they did. You'd be thinking about them all day."

I nod. "I would have, yes. And probably have broken my silence asking if you had received them."

Marjorie leans over, and we kiss. "Thank you. They were a lovely surprise."

We return to our own thoughts for a moment. Marjorie takes a book from her bag, and I turn back to the window.

The conductor walks by, we show our tickets and return to our reverie, which is only broken by the regular stops at towns of varying sizes and passengers. Fortunately, the space around us remains unoccupied.

"Did you think about lunch?"

Marjorie puts her book down and turns to me. "Yes. I think the hotel sounds nice. Let's meet there."

I nod. "Okay. My meeting shouldn't be more than a couple of hours."

"I have some shopping to do."

"I can meet you when you're done. We can walk to the hotel."

"Or take a taxi."

"Or take a taxi. That might be a good idea."

"We'll play it by ear."

"I don't want to hurry you. We'll see how it goes."

"I'm already hungry."

"Really? I laugh. I told you to buy a bun before we left."

Marjorie wrinkles her nose. "I know. I wanted to wait."

"All morning?"

"I had a large breakfast." She sighs. "I'm gaining too much weight."

I look at her, though I needn't. I think she's the most beautiful woman in the world. "You *are* getting a bit plump." I lie, chuckle, and turn back to the window just before Marjorie hits me with her paperback.

"Swine!"

I turn to her. "I've known you thin, fat, and all the variations in between. I've known your face now and fifteen years younger. I love each iteration."

She sits back, pouting. "I know. That's the worst of it. It doesn't matter what I do or wear; you find me irresistible."

"I'm a horrible person."

"You are."

"I'll try to be like other men."

"Do try." Marjorie laughs. "Be more demanding. You don't even mind if I wear makeup or not."

"I think you're beautiful with and without makeup."

"Exactly. You don't care. You're impossible."

"I'm a bad man." I smile and return to my window, lifting the cup to my mouth and emptying the last sips of coffee. Holding it at an angle in my hand against the window, I take a photo with my phone, adjust the filter, and set it up on my Instagram account. #Thursday. #CoffeetoGo.

"You forgot a sustainability hashtag."

I put down my phone. "I was thinking about that, but I don't want to overdo it." I turn. "I want to write a post about sustainability. I'll use the photo then. I don't know. Sustainability seems a bit deep." I look back out the window. "I was looking for something simpler."

Marjorie returns to her book. I look back over at her. "What were you thinking of eating?"

She looks up. "For lunch? I've no idea. It's still a few hours away."

"You said you were hungry. I thought you might be having cravings."

Marjorie raises her eyebrows. "Cravings?"

"Fish. Meat. Dumplings. Something Asian. Ice cream."

"Ice cream and dumplings? I'm not pregnant, and you know I'm vegetarian, so meat won't fly."

I smile. "Yes, yes, of course. I meant, sort of, variations of food. The hotel has three restaurants. I was thinking about a clubhouse sandwich."

"I'll probably have pasta."

I nod. "That's always a good choice."

"Without any meat. Or pickles."

I smile. "Even better."

After an uneventful hour, the train slows, crossing the iron bridge that spans the first of the many canals that spread through the city like so many tentacles.

The train slows down even further, sliding into the station as if for the first time, wary and unsure if it will fit into the covered platforms filled with people and bags. Over the loudspeaker, we are reminded to take our belongings.

I help Marjorie on with her coat if for no other reason than to hold her shoulders for a moment, feel her warmth and inhale her spicy scent before stepping outside into the cold air.

"Shall I walk with you to the shop? Or …"

"I'll be fine. You can take the metro from here. It's faster."

I look at my watch. "Hmm, you're right. I'd better get a move on." I look up and smile. "Though Peter will be late. He always is."

Marjorie laughs. "He wouldn't be Peter if he weren't late."

She takes my arm and raises herself up on her toes to kiss me. "You'd be meeting a stranger if he were on time."

I laugh. "That's true."

She holds on to my arm for a moment longer. "I'll call you when I'm done. We can decide where we meet then. I'll probably be about two hours, though."

Marjorie nods, releases my arm and takes a step backwards. "Fine." She smiles. "Say hello from me."

I raise my hand and begin walking backwards. "I will!"

"I'm looking forward to lunch!" She calls, smiles, and turns, then walks briskly away.

I stand for a few moments and watch her go, bundled in her long, red jacket, pants tucked into her high black boots, black hat pulled tightly down on her head. Just that, but it makes my stomach jump in an oddly pleasurable way like she's attached by a string that pulls tighter as she walks away.

margarida

I open the door, feeling the weight of something nudging and then crumpling as I push the door inwards. My keys jangle in the lock, and I peer down.

"It's okay! It's just newspaper!" I hear Margarida's voice before I see her face, her footsteps growing louder as she comes to the door and pulls it inwards.

"Hi!" Her long grey-black hair, stuck to her face in places, billows about her shoulders. Her face is slightly wet, and a finger length of clay runs from her nose to her cheek. "How was your day?"

"Hi, back." I look down at the newspapers crumpling around my feet as I enter. "It was fine. Busy. The usual." She pushes the door closed behind me, and I lean over to kiss her. "You've been busy today."

"You've no idea!" She turns and retreats back down the hallway into her studio, raising her arms in the air. Her thick indoor slippers scatter the newspaper as she walks. "Sorry about the mess!" She calls from the back room. "I thought I was on to something."

I take off my jacket, hang it behind the door, and walk the length of the hallway, peering into her studio.

"I was … but it all went wrong. I don't know. I've got it now, though."

Margarida sits at her potter's wheel, a fan slowly turning beside her. Clumps of clay of varying sizes are arranged about the studio on plinths and side tables. Not a little seems to have been traipsed around on the floor. Ah. Hence the newspapers.

"It sort of got out of control."

I nod. "How about a cup of tea?" I raise my arm. "I brought buns."

"That would be lovely."

I nod and turn towards the door. "Be careful in the kitchen." I turn back to her. "It's not confined to this room."

I walk uncertainly into the kitchen, where my worst fears are confirmed. "It is … it *did* get away from you!" I call back. There are clay pots of various sizes and stages of completion on almost every inch of counter and tabletop. "Didn't it?" I say to myself.

I gently move one of the objets d'art, pick up the kettle, and fill it with water. Then I plug it in and reach into the cupboard for teacups and tea. Earl Grey. Milk, no lemon.

While I wait for the water to boil, I walk back to the studio, with a detour to the living room and the bedroom, which both, thankfully, appear untouched by the artistic carnage.

I peer around the door. "What happened then?"

Margarida runs her wet, clay-covered hands over the quickly spinning object on the wheel in front of her. The skin above her nose is pressed tightly between her fine, black brows as she frowns, and focuses, shapes and caresses the object before her into life.

After a few minutes, the velocity of the wheel reduces, her brows return to their natural place above her eyes, and smiling, she sits back, wiping the back of her hand over her forehead, leaving a thick swatch of grey-brown clay.

She looks up. "Sorry?" She takes a cloth from her pocket and wipes her face.

The kettle begins to whistle me back to the kitchen. "I'll be back."

I return a few minutes later with two cups of tea and a small plate on which two sticky sweet buns sit upon a napkin. Margarida clears a small space on the desk beside her. "Thank you."

"You're welcome." I look at the pot on the wheel she is gently carving into with a metal ring attached to a wooden stick. "I was asking, what happened?" I look around. "This explosion of … of creativity."

She laughs. "You mean what the fuck is all this mess?"

I take a sip from my tea. "That would be another way of putting it, yes."

She wipes her hands on her pants and reaches over for her cup, drinking it with her eyes on me.

"You're sweet."

"I have that fault."

Margarida guffaws, spilling tea as she exhales. "One of your many."

"I am nothing but not richly endowed."

"I might have to run for a bucket."

"You *know* what I mean."

She laughs, takes up one of the buns and bites into it. "Mmm, this is yummy. Thank you. I haven't eaten anything all day."

"Because you were busy doing … ?"

"I got a job!"

"Aha! Nice! That would explain all your … clay."

"Yes! The library wants me to make pots. Well, I don't exactly know how many, but I wanted to be prepared." She takes another sip of tea and a final bite of her bun. "For a show." Chewing, she looks around her studio, nodding and swallowing. "They want them by next month. I'm trying to find my stride."

I blink. "I thought you had brought home a stray from the shelter."

She frowns, looking at me.

"The newspapers all over the floor."

Margarida laughs. "Ah! I see. No. No strays."

I look around. "Thinking of that, where are the girls?" I hadn't seen any of Margarida's three cats since my arrival.

"I think I frightened them off. All the paper, the spinning, the screaming."

"Screaming?" I raise my eyebrows and move some books from a small wooden stool onto the floor before sitting down.

"I had the most beautiful hydria before my hand slipped, and I took off the top." She looks at me, questioningly reaching for the second bun.

"That must have been frustrating. I'm sorry." I nod and smile.

She chews contently. "I'll have a bath in a few minutes. The girls will come out of their hiding places once I've stopped. They always do."

"So, we're still on for dinner?" I asked, relieved.

"Of course. I've been looking forward to it all week."

"One year together."

"Too many years apart."

"Little wins."

Margarida nods. "You're right." She stands up and looks me up and down. "Are you going like that?"

I stand up, looking myself up and down. "Why?"

"You look fine. I was just gauging what I should wear." She picks up the empty plate and her cup, and I follow her out into the hallway then to the kitchen.

"Wear your purple dress. I love that."

"Really?" She places her cup and the plate in the sink, reaches out and takes my cup.

"Really."

She leans over and kisses me. She smells amazing. Rich and earthy. She smells of dust and water, clay and sweat. "Then I'll wear that."

"I'm going to get ready." She walks out of the kitchen, stops in the hallway and calls for her cats. "If you love me, you might bag up all this paper." She turns back smiles at me.

"Ah. I *do* love you, so I guess I'm stuck." I smile and turn to the corner of the studio where a large box of industrial garbage bags sit.

margarethe

Margarethe's hands skillfully move the risotto about the pan, catching the small globules of butter softened garlic and onion until each kernel is coated. The sounds of the stirring reminiscent of a spade digging its way into a bucket of gravel, that thoughts of childhood spring to mind. Summer afternoons on hot beaches. Fingers sticky with melted ice cream and hurriedly applied sun lotion.

The hot pan angrily barks as she pours in a glass of white wine, followed by another of chicken stock, constantly stirring with her free hand.

"You do that so well."

Margarethe looks over and smiles. "Thank you." She places the cover on the pan and reduces the heat. "Do you want another glass of wine?"

I stand up and walk over to her, holding my glass steady as she pours the cold, golden, liquid. "It's a nice wine." I lift the glass to my nose, inhale, and take a sip.

"Gewürztraminer goes well with risotto."

"Dinner *and* wine advice all in one evening."

"Smartass." Margarethe kicks me playfully, smiling. "Sit."

Margarethe's mushroom risotto is a dream. The right amount of hard, grated cheese, the correct amount of freshly hacked tarragon, the perfect number of small, bright green peas.

Unlike Margarethe, I'm not vegetarian. Nor am I vegan. Nor strictly carnivorous, for that matter. I can eat pretty much whatever you put in front of me. Growing up in the suburbs, I ate the standard meat, starch, and vegetable dinners, probably like most of the people in our neighbourhood. I don't remember seeing a vegetarian restaurant until I grew up and lived in the city.

Vegetarian restaurants struck me as mysterious and possibly dangerous, and there was something unnatural about people who only ate vegetables. It didn't help that during the 60s and 70s, such restaurants were usually found in the less upscale parts of the city. Now, of course, they have come of age. Vegan and vegetarian restaurants flourish in high-end quarters while meat-eaters are looked upon askance.

As the years went by, sometimes by accident and sometimes out of necessity, meat played less of a role in my meals. There were Asian ramen, Italian pasta, and a world of salads, soups, and sandwiches that were amply filling and excitingly delicious despite being meatless. After Margarethe and I met and began eating together regularly, I ate what she ate, and she never rebuked me for ordering a ribeye steak or salmon when we ate out. And honestly, we often both order a pasta dish anyway. We have had many disagreements, but not one of them has been about food or drink.

I watch her as she slices the mushrooms in slow, precise movements. Her compact form works protectively close to the cutting board.

"I'm going to give you something to do." She looks over at me a few times. She smiles and wipes her hands and then walks to the refrigerator. I smile and drink my wine, contentedly watching her.

"I am doing something. I'm looking at you."

"I know." Margarethe laughs. "And you're making me nervous."

I watch as she removes a head of lettuce, small cucumbers, and a misshapen red bell pepper, clutching them in her arms and pushing the door closed with her shoulder. She places everything into the sink and, after sniffing the tomatoes to find the ripest, adds three tomatoes from the windowsill to the pile forming beneath the running water.

She returns to her post by the chopping board as the water runs. "You were a chef, I believe?"

"Right! Of course. Sorry. I thought you wanted to do it all yourself."

I place my hand on her shoulder and gently squeeze as I walk to the sink, turn off the water, and reach for a cutting board and knife.

"I do. You can prepare the salad, though."

"Happy to."

She turns to me and smiles. I'm prepared to work long hours if she pays me in smiles.

The kitchen resonates with the tearing of lettuce and the slicing of fresh vegetables on one side, and the grating and chopping of finer delicacies on the other. Another thirty minutes, and dinner, as they say, is served.

Margarethe's risotto is a thing of beauty. A lot of risotto I've had is either porridge or sticky rice. You've probably had the same experience. Margarethe cooks hers slowly and evenly. If possible, she caresses each grain until it reaches the perfect tenderness. It's the one dish she seems completely at home with, which is probably why it always turns out so good.

"Mmm." After finishing my second helping, I sit back and reach for my glass of wine. "That was so good. Again. Always."

Margarethe smiles, reddening slightly perhaps, her eyes twinkling. "I'm glad you liked it."

"I did."

"Do you have room for dessert?"

I sip from my glass and open my eyes wide in surprise. "Dessert?"

"Don't get too excited." She laughs, reaching over for my plate, and adding it to hers. "Some fruit." She stands up and takes our plates and cutlery to the sink. "And I have some cheese."

"That sounds perfect." I finish my wine, stand up and take my glass to the sink. I place my arm around her waist and kiss her. "Thank you. It was absolutely delicious."

I walk to the refrigerator and reach for the door handle. "No. Sit down." Margarethe follows me, puts her hands on my shoulders and gently points me toward the table. "You've helped enough."

I raise my hands in surrender. "Okay. As you wish." I return to my chair, cross one leg over the other, lean back and watch her remove cheese from the refrigerator. "Find something to do other than watch me." She says with her back turned to me.

I laugh. "Okay." I take up my phone that is sitting on the table. "I'll check my mails."

Margarethe nods. "That sounds fine."

I scroll through my emails and messages, one eye on the screen and the other on Margarethe.

"I can feel you looking."

I roll my eyes, stand up, and leave the kitchen. "I'm going to the balcony. If I can't look at the stars in your eyes, I'll look into the heavens."

Margarethe shrieks her amusement as I walk to the living room. "No more wine for you!" Her laugh follows me outside.

Margarethe's building, situated on a hill, offers a good view of the neighbourhood, which, if not there, would be a good view of the fields and the river in the distance. The second-floor apartment's long balcony wraps around so that I can exit from one door, walk around the corner of the living room, and reenter through a different one. Apartments are often such a box; one way in, one way out. This design was probably not a deciding factor when Margarethe took the apartment, but it's one I immediately appreciated.

I scroll back through my emails and messages, deleting most, but saving a few for later perusal. When email first came into my house, 'you have mail' was a rare and exciting treat. We never received anywhere near as many letters or phone calls before mobile phones arrived. Even getting a call on my first 'brick' phone was a special occasion. Now we receive dozens of electronic messages at all times of the day and night and think no more of them than the junk mail that used to fill our letter box each morning.

"Well?" Margarethe walks out the door and onto the balcony, her arms crossed in front of her, wrapping in the warmth. "I thought you were star gazing."

I lower my phone and laugh, looking up to the sky. "Honestly, the stars are nothing compared to looking at you."

She bumps up against me and then raises herself for a kiss. Our lips press lightly together, and I inhale her aroma and that of the meal. "Mm, you smell good."

"Thank you. Dessert is almost ready. The cheese is just warming up."

"Time for another kiss?"

"Perhaps." Margarethe presses herself against me. "Put your phone away and hold me."

I place my phone in my back pocket and take her in my arms, pressing her close. She nestles against me. "Mm, this is nice. Hold me tighter."

"Tighter?" I laugh. "You'll have to climb into me to be any closer."

Margarethe looks up, and we kiss. "That would be nice. Being inside of you, warm and safe."

"Until I start jogging. Then you'll be bumping up and down. Horrible."

She laughs. "You never go jogging."

"I may start at any moment."

"You just don't want to carry me."

"I'm only concerned about my own weight."

Margarethe laughs and withdraws. "Ha! Your moment has come and gone. 'You would be, but a feather' was the correct response to any suggestion about my weight." She walks back towards the door, raising her hands above her. "Too heavy to jog with. Insults on an evening like this."

I follow her inside, grabbing her about the waist and gently turning her around. "A feather would be hardly noticed. Would you want that?" She smiles, looks away, and playfully tries to break free of my embrace.

"Words. Just words."

"Thoughts of you weigh me down like no boulder."

"Ohh!" She lets herself go limp in my arms. "Your sugary tongue has pierced me. I breathe no more."

She hangs limp in my arms, her weight – ever so slight, of course - making me fall over so that we collapse onto the couch together, laughing hysterically.

We lay there running our fingers gently over each other's faces. "I love you."

Margarethe closes her eyes, reopening them, smiling deeply. "I love you too."

margriet

"What's the difference between homeopathy and, say, healing with herbs? Flowers and things. Or say healing with other natural elements. Naturopathy. Warm stones or hot sand? They have that in Japan, don't they? People go to spas and lay covered in hot volcanic sand?"

Margriet laughs. "Sand bathing. Yes. I've heard of it." She carries a stack of magazines to the hallway and places them in one of the many open cardboard boxes. "Don't move any of the piles I've made."

"What if you've missed something?"

She returns to the living room, where I am flipping through a battered paperback that I've taken from one of the piles arranged on the desk.

She smiles, taking the book gently from my hands. "I know you. You'll move things. I've spent all morning sorting out the things I don't want to take with me."

"We have so much space in the new apartment."

"It will be nice to have space to move about in."

"I'm just afraid you'll give a book away, and then, oops, it's gone."

"I'll order it again if that happens."

"I don't know. I think you should take them all."

"Never. There are books here I should have gotten rid of years ago." She picks one up and holds it in front of me. "Build Your Own Website in FrontPage. How often will I need this again?" She lifts another. "Charcuterie for the Modern Woman." She rolls her eyes, places them back on the pile, and carries this into the hallway.

"The first one would be a nice museum piece. I have books from the dawn of the internet. They're fun to look back at." I walk over to the window and look out across the rooftops. "Why you have a book on charcuterie is beyond me." I turn and walk towards the hallway as she returns. "Haven't you always been vegetarian?"

She smiles. "It was a gift from a student."

"Hmm." I nod. "You didn't answer my question."

"I thought you were trying to be funny. I've explained it to you before." She passes me going into the other room. "You never let me treat you. Why are you interested, anyway?"

"Oh, not true! I took the preparation you gave me when I damaged my finger."

Margriet pops her head around the doorframe. "That was more than ten years ago. At least." She disappears again.

"Well… you know me. I'm entrenched in western medicine. I don't even like taking aspirin unless I've got a fever. A high fever." I qualify my remark by raising my voice.

Margriet returns to the living room. "Now you're yelling at me." She shakes her head and tuts jokingly.

"Sorry. I thought you were in the next room."

I lift a book in my hand. "The book on herbs and flowers reminded me to ask again." I nod to the book, placing it back on the table.

Margriet picks it up and flips through the pages. "Ah! I remember this book. I bought it when I was still at university. Some of us had a flower garden. I thought it would be interesting." She puts it back down. "I haven't opened it for years."

"A good treasure. To take with you. A reminder of school and everything."

She lifts another stack of books and walks back into the hallway. "How many books from university do you still have?"

I sit down in one of the chairs, facing the coffee table and other stacks of books, papers, and magazines. "Probably only two. Both copies of a student journal I contributed poetry to." I laugh. "I don't even have any of my textbooks left. They cost a fortune too."

Margriet returns. "I rest my case."

"So unfair. The kids get them all online these days. They don't even have to carry them. Look, are you sure there isn't anything I can do to help you?"

"You could make some coffee? Please? That would be nice."

I stand up quickly. "I'm on the job," I announce with excited seriousness.

"You're funny."

"I'm happy to be of some amusement to you." I kiss her on the cheek as I pass and head into the kitchen.

Margriet's voice follows me. "You amuse me daily."

I roll my eyes and smile, enter the kitchen and look about for the coffee percolator. After lifting a few things, I find it behind a box of plates. While I prepare the coffee, Margriet brings another stack of paper into the hallway, dropping it carefully into a box. She walks into the kitchen and sits at the small wooden table. "Not too strong for me, please."

"Of course." I pour some milk into a metal jug, placing it on another element set to low.

"I need to sit down for a bit. All that lifting."

I turn and smile at her. "All those books. Wise woman."

Margriet snorts. "To answer your question, again, there is a bit of a crossover. Homeopathy is often used in naturopathy. The remedies are developed from natural substances. Small doses are given to enhance the body's natural ability to heal.

Homeopathy works on the theory that 'like cures like', which means something that gives a healthy person symptoms should cure the same symptoms for someone who is ill."

I nod, watching her as she talks.

"Naturopathy, on the other hand, believes nature has a healing power all its own. It takes a holistic and natural approach to the body's ability to heal and maintain health and wellbeing."

I nod again.

"I have no idea about hot sand and stones, other than they're probably relaxing. The rest is all on my website." She raises an eyebrow and smiles.

"Really. Sorry. I was just questioning out loud."

She gets up and walks over to me, wrapping her arms around my waist and hugging me. "I love you."

I hold her tightly. "I love you too."

"Ah!" The sound of the percolator bubbling coffee to the top of the glass spout separates us.

I remove the percolator from the element. "Would you like a cappuccino, or … ?"

Margriet already has the small, electric, milk whisk in her hand. "Please."

As Margriet whisks the warm milk into a frothy foam, I take out two cups from the cupboard and fill them half full with coffee.

"Cookie?" I look around. "The cookie jar is packed?"

Margriet nods her head. "No cookies for me. You go ahead, though."

I look about the kitchen. "Um … where are they?"

Margriet laughs, walking over to a collection of foodstuffs next to the refrigerator. Among bananas, cereal boxes, grape clusters, and a loaf of bread, she reaches in and brings out a half-open package of chocolate digestives.

"Ooh, chocolate." I take one from the package she offers me. "Thank you."

I pass her a coffee cup, which she takes in both hands, holding it close to her chest. "Thank you for coming by to help. There's more to do than I expected."

"You've been here a long time." I smile, sipping my coffee and finishing my cookie. "Happy?"

Margriet nods. "Yes, in a way. I'll miss this place and everything that happened here." She looks around the kitchen and then back to me. "I'm looking forward to being together in the new flat. It's going to be an adventure."

"A good one, I hope!" I laugh, and she joins me.

"You know, it will be the last place we live in. We'll be old together. It's funny thinking about it."

I snort. "I'm old now! But I know what you mean. I'm looking forward to being together. And I'm oddly excited. It's strange. I should be terrified, knowing this is the last move, but I feel excited too. We're going to be together. It took so long, but it's finally happening."

Margriet nods. "Yes." She looks at me with a mixture of sadness and amusement. "It did take a very long time."

"I'm sorry."

She shakes her head. "No. It's not your fault. Not completely. We've both changed a lot since we first met. There is no guarantee we would have been happy or stayed together had we lived together earlier. Maybe it took this long for us to be completely ready."

I finish my coffee. "I think it was mostly my fault, but you're kind saying that."

"Don't try to steal all the spotlight for yourself. You know I was difficult."

"I could have been less so. More mature. I don't know. I've never really grown up." I chuckle. "I'm a bit of a swine, actually. I feel as though I am anyway."

"Stop. You're not. I know our past hasn't been the smoothest, but we're both together now, and the years ahead of us will be better because they were so long and difficult in coming."

"I read that we put off committing to things we want out of fear of no longer wanting them once we've jumped on board."

Margriet shrugs. "There's probably something to that." She looks at me. "You wrote that in an article, didn't you?"

I look at her sheepishly. "Is it too horrid quoting myself?"

"Beyond the pale." She gives me a pained smile. "Come on. I've got a lot of packing still to do."

margisia

I watch her shuffling the cards, trying not to look too closely. She shuffles, looking across at me. I look away. She breaks the cards into three piles and divides the cards between them. I turn my attention again to her face. I always let her shuffle so that I can watch her. She looks up again.
"You're going to make me make a mistake."

"A mistake? Shuffling the cards?"

"I have a system. I need to concentrate. You're distracting me."

"I can go into the next room."

"No. Stay here. I feel alone when you're not here."

I reach out and take Margisia's warm hand in mine. The skin of her fingers, roughened over the years, still feels so soft to the touch. Perhaps I'm biased, but I love holding it.

She laughs. "How can I shuffle if you're holding one of my hands?"

I raise my hands in defeat. "I'll get myself a glass of wine. Leave you in peace."

"Thank you."

I stand up and place my hands on her shoulders, leaning over to kiss her cheek.

"Can I bring you anything?"

"I'm fine."

I pour myself a glass of red wine and lean against the counter, watching her.

"You can come back now." She says as she deals the cards.

I sit down and pick up the cards as they appear on the table in front of me. "Who dealt this mess?"

Margisia laughs.

"You needn't have bothered shuffling."

"You can shuffle next time."

"No, no. You do it. I like watching you."

"I told you that distracts me. That's why you got such bad cards."

I wouldn't say I like playing cards, but I like spending long, quiet moments with her. I like how she looks over the rims of her glasses at her cards. I like the set of her mouth as she considers which cards to keep and which to discard. I like the opportunity to look at her while she is otherwise distracted. You could say I am in love with her, and you would not be wrong.

Decided, Margisia takes three cards and places them on the table in front of her. "Three tens." She follows this with three other cards. "Three, four, and five." She then places a card on the discard pile. "A stop card for you, so I get to draw again." She takes the top card from the downturned stack in front of us, looks at it for some time, and then slides it in between the three remaining cards in her hand. "Three, four, five, six." She places the six of hearts next to the other three cards in the sequence. "And a discard." She places a nine on the discard pile. "That leaves me with two cards." She smiles at me. "Your turn."

I look at her, then down at her cards, and back to the ten cards fanned out in my hand. I see no chance to put down any card. "It's really no fun playing with you." I chuckle.

Margisia giggles and places her free hand on top my mine. "I'm sorry."

"I don't think you are at all." I frown slightly, take a card from the deck, peer at it, then over at those laid out in front of her. Useless. I breathe in deeply and exhale, placing the card face up on the discard stack. As I expected, she greedily picks it up before it has a chance to settle. "Out!"

I close my eyes and shake my head, hoping to clear my incomprehension. "Um, how?"

She has taken my discarded two and placed it behind the three, along with an ace which she had been holding, finally discarding an unnecessary eight.

"The two before the three. How did you miss it?"

I blink slowly and stare at the cards. How *did* I miss it?

"I'm not good at card games."

"You need to focus more."

"I do. You're too good."

"You spend too much time looking at me instead of the cards."

"Guilty as charged."

"Another round?"

I look over to the tally sheet. "How much am I down?"

Margisia quickly tallies the numbers. "One hundred and twelve." She looks over at me.

"Any chance of my catching up tonight?"

"None." She smiles.

"Then why don't we watch something."

She nods. "That would be nice. Would you like some more wine?"

I look at my empty glass, then over to the bottle on the counter. "Is there any left?"

Margisia places the cards together then pushes them into the box. She gets up, straightens her skirt and walks to the counter. Lifting the bottle, she peers through the dark green glass, tilting it slightly. "Very little. Finish it off. I'm good."

I stand up and hold out my glass as she empties the remaining Bardolino wine into it. "It was really quite good."

Margisia stoppers the bottle and puts it on the counter near the sink. "It was. I'll have to remember to buy another bottle when I'm at the store."

"Want anything?" I ask, looking around the kitchen.

"No. I'm fine." She takes my arm. "Full."

We walk out of the kitchen and down the hallway into the living room. "You shouldn't let me beat you at cards like that." Margisia walks over to the television, turns it on, returning with the remote control in her hand. She drops onto the sofa and points the device at the screen.

"I was honestly *not* trying to let you beat me." I sit down next to her. She removes her slippers and curls her bare feet up beside her, pressing them up against my thigh.

"My feet are cold. Would you mind?"

I lift my leg slightly so she can slide her feet beneath.

"Mmm, thank you."

"I love you."

She pushes herself up from the pillows, and we kiss. "I love you too." She smiles and then drops back down.

Margisia points the remote at the television and clicks through a few channels before asking me what we should watch. I'm a fairly open-minded viewer and will politely watch anything someone chooses. Most of the time. Some of the nonsense that is produced for which we are expected to sacrifice even forty minutes of our existence is honestly shocking. I want to meet some of the families with whom the networks test their programming. Now *that* would be entertainment.

Downton Abbey begins and ends over the next hour, the backdrop for comments, questions, and laughs on her side and mine. My penchant for looking at Margisia is made easier by her concentration on the exploits of Edith and Gregson playing out on the screen in front of us. I haven't grown tired of looking at her face in all the years we've been together.

"Did you enjoy it?" She removes her feet from beneath me and leans over, kissing me and wrapping herself over me like a blanket.

"Oof! Yes, I did." I chuckle. "Did you?"

"I did. But I meant did you enjoy looking at me, silly." She kisses me again.

"I did. Yes. I'd much rather look at you than the television."

Margisia laughs and looks at her watch. "You're crazy. It's getting late. Let's go to bed."

marjatta

"Slow down, please?"

"I thought you liked walking."

"You know I do. I can't walk as fast nor as well as I used to."

I slow down my stride, and Marjatta takes my arm in hers. "There. Is that better?"

I wrap my arm around her waist and pull her close, kissing the top of her head through her wind-swept hair. "Of course, it is."

We walk slowly, without any destination in mind, enjoying the wildflowers and the smells of the sea hidden behind the dike that runs away into the distance. When we see a bench, we stop and rest, my arm around her shoulders and her head pressed against my chest.

There being no big demand for Tinder among the elderly, we are always given the benefit of the doubt when people wonder how long we have been together. If you passed us by, you might think, 'Even now, they are still very much in love.'

Marjatta looks up, and we kiss. "Shall we go back? To the hotel?"

"Where else would we go?"

"The café was nice."

"It really was. You're right." I look left and right along the path that seems to go on forever in both directions. "I liked the grilled cheese sandwich. With the pickle."

Marjatta sits up. "We could go back for cake. And tea."

"What about the hotel?"

She smiles. "If we go back to the hotel, you'll just seduce me back into bed."

"That would be … terrible."

She laughs. "Incredibly so. But I'm still sore from last night."

"I'm sorry."

"I'm getting old."

"So am I." I take her hand in mine and squeeze it gently. "And I love you exactly as you are, so don't get any ideas about becoming any younger."

Marjatta laughs, then turns to look out across the fields, thinking and watching. "Men can probably do it until their dying day." She looks back at me. "Survival of the species." She reaches over and takes my hands in her. "Women … we dry up."

"It doesn't seem at all fair."

"There are young women available to old men."

"I don't want young women. I want you."

She smiles and squeezes my hands firmly. "You're saying I'm old?" She laughs before I can respond. "I know what you mean. Thank you."

"I love holding you. Kissing your lips. Looking at your face. Feeling you pressed against me." I tenderly run my finger over her cheek. "It's incredibly satisfying."

"Mmm, I like that too."

"You're right, though. We should have something more to eat. We'll be starving by the time we get back."

She nods.

"We're in bed together each night anyway." I stand up and hold out my hands, gently helping her up from the bench. "It's the highlight of my day. Just you and I, alone in the darkness."

"You should never have left the greeting card business." Marjatta laughs as we fall into step, returning in the direction we had come.

"I was never *in* the greeting card business." I laugh.

"Then you missed your calling."

We walk slowly back to the village, hand in hand, sometimes exchanging glances, mostly happy to just be alone together as the sun dips inch by inch into the horizon.

The lights of the café are visible as we cross the last field between us and much-needed calories.

"I didn't realise how far we had walked."

"It's too late for cake."

"Can it ever be too late for cake?"

She laughs, and I look at my watch. "It's almost five."

"It *is* too late for cake then."

Across the street from the café, our hotel beckons invitingly. "Why don't we rest, have a bath, and go for dinner? In an hour?"

Marjatta nods. "That's probably a good idea. I need to soak my feet."

"I can massage them for you if you like."

She guffaws. "You only like massaging my feet because you think it will lead to sex."

"There is that." I wink at her as we walk across the street to our hotel.

"You're setting your sights too high tonight." I pull open the front door and hold it for her.

"Nothing ventured, nothing gained as they say."

Marjatta reaches back and takes my hand, leading me across the lobby. "Good evening!" The hotel staff are friendly and eager to please.

"Good evening!"

As we wait for the elevator to the third floor, Marjatta leans into me and kisses me tenderly. "I love you."

I smile warmly, looking into her eyes. "I love you too."

The elevator arrives, the doors open, and we step inside.

"Let's shower and go for an early dinner." She holds my hand in hers. "I'll soak in the bath when we return. If I don't fall asleep, maybe, you'll get lucky."

I laugh. "In that case, I'm not going to order dessert."

"You have a one-track mind. I should never have married you." She laughs, the melody rich and deep.

"Ah, but you did." I lean over and kiss her. "And I'm very glad you said yes."

Marjatta and I were the oldest couple the justice of the peace had ever married in all his years tying couples together. Shortly after the ceremony, four years ago, on an early summer afternoon, we had driven out to this same hotel for our honeymoon. It wasn't the first hotel we had stayed in together, but it was the first one as husband and wife.

I suppose if we had been younger, we would have opted for brighter lights and bigger cities, imaginative meals and social media-friendly backdrops, but all we wanted was to be together.

We had visited the quiet waterfront town together once before by chance and decided it would be the best place to enjoy all the lost minutes we had missed being apart. We were greedy for those hours and were happy not to waste them with anything other than ourselves.

Marjatta and I agree on some things, but not everything. Eating in or near your hotel is one of those things we usually both agree not to do, but after a few visits, we returned to the café for almost every meal on each of our trips.

'Proximity to the marriage bed' Marjatta had chuckled when we ate our first meal in the small café located across the street from the hotel. After that lunch of scrambled eggs and toasted bread heavy with grains and thickly spread with butter and strawberry jam, we quickly returned to the still-warm bed. Wrapped in the thick sheets, our noses pressed gently against each other as we kissed and caressed, our mouths still pleasantly tasting of eggs and butter and toast.

"I thought if we married, I'd finally have some peace." Marjatta had laughed. "Where do you get the energy?"

"I can't help it. You arouse and inspire me." I had kissed her deep red lips for the hundredth time that day. "You're beautiful, and I love you."

She had stroked my face and smiled contently. "We should have done this years ago."

I had smiled, my roguish grin, which preceded most of what I imagined was witty and charming. "I wasn't convinced when we first met. You weren't nearly as beautiful then." Marjatta had laughed and playfully pushed my face away. "It's true!" I had tried to laugh my way out of it, and then she had pulled me against her, and we had made love in our familiar way long into the afternoon.

"What are you thinking?" Marjatta's voice recalls me back to my meal, the chatter and murmurs of the café surrounding me once more.

I smile, blink, and reach for my glass of wine. "The first time we ate here. The late morning after our wedding night."

Marjatta nods and smiles. "We had scrambled eggs. You were still strong and fit."

Swallowing my wine just in time, I laugh out loud. "You weren't as beautiful." I wink. "But you were somewhat pretty."

We both laugh; Marjatta sits back, sips from her water glass and looks at me. "Happy?"

"Very." I spear a piece of my fish and look at it. "I could be happier with the fish, though." I place it in my mouth and chew thoughtfully. "It used to be better."

Marjatta laughs and returns to her meal. "You're losing your sense of taste. Mine is wonderful."

I look over at her wild mushroom fettucini. "You don't have the fish."

She raises an eyebrow, nodding, placing pasta and sauce into her mouth, then wiping her lips with a starched white napkin. "There is that." She chews and swallows. "But you have complained before about not tasting things."

"Thankfully, I can still taste you." I smile.

"Hahaha! Oh my. Does this charm of yours work on your girlfriends, or do you save it all for me?" Marjatta laughs, crossing her cutlery on her now empty plate.

I decide against finishing my fish, signalling to the waiter that I, too, am done with my meal. I wipe my mouth with my napkin, chuckling and shaking my head. "No, no, it's all for you, my dear. My girlfriends have all long since despaired of me. It's all for you."

Marjatta rolls her eyes and snorts. "How did I get so lucky?" She looks about. "Wasn't there a dessert cart when we came in?"

"For someone so sweet?"

"Stop it!" She playfully reprimands me. "Yes. That's how I stay so sweet by eating desserts. I want to see what they have. And you?"

I shake my head. "I'm fine with my wine. You enjoy."

Two waiters, signalled by our mostly empty plates, converge on our table, one clearing our table while Marjatta sends the other in search of the dessert cart.

Marjatta's cheesecake and fresh strawberries embolden me to order a whisky. In contented silence, we sit together as the café slowly fills with later dinner guests.

"That was delicious." Marjatta licks her fork. "Let's go back to the hotel."

I signal to the waiter, signing my name in the air. "You can have your soak in the bath."

"And you can massage my feet."

"It seems like there's something for everyone."

I sign the bill and take Marjatta's hand in mine. "Shall we?"

Like So Many Pearls Before a Swine: A Love Story

Margot
Margaret
Marjorie
Margarida

part one **two** three

Margarethe
Margriet
Margisia
Marjatta

margot

"C'est la chambre 169. Oui. Pourriez-vous nous apporter des serviettes supplémentaires? Merci." Margot replaces her earring and puts down the phone. "They always skimp on towels." She shakes her head, walking over to the table where I am sorting through the wines we've purchased. "I suppose it pays out in the end."

"Probably." I make a few notes in my notebook. "If the towels aren't there, you can't use them."

Margit picks up a half bottle of Ehrenfelser, turning it in the light. "Well. It's nice they fit the bed with two sets of sheets."

I laugh. "Yes. Though, I would have no issue with laying together on one set." I look up. "Or sharing a single bed."

"Mmm. We've done that enough. Remember the day bed in Leipzig?" We both laugh. "I honestly thought we'd be spending the entire long weekend on that thing."

"I like their label. Shiny." Margot replaces the bottle on the table. "I like the smaller bottles too. Very practical."

I nod. "Two glasses. Ideal if you don't want to open an entire bottle."

"Why didn't you leave the wine in the car? It's locked in the garage."

"Well, I wanted to see what I'm missing for one. I didn't want the chance that the car was broken into either."

"True. Foreign plates, nice sports car, incredibly sexy female passenger." Margot nods.

"Now, that *was* my biggest concern. Which is why I brought you up to the room and didn't let you sit in the car overnight." I laugh, reaching out and pulling her down onto my lap.

"Hahaha! You swine." Margot struggles lightly to stand up and then kisses me deeply. "Mmm, I love you, but I think you love wine more."

"Well, I can drink the wine. I can only look at you."

"You said I tasted so good last night …" Margot raises an eyebrow high on her face.

"And, of course, a few other things." I laugh and release her.

"Shall we go? We're meeting Rachel and Tom in Basel for lunch, don't forget."

"It's a forty-minute drive from here. We just had breakfast."

"I know you. We'll stop at this winery and that winery to admire this grape and that grape."

"There's the Ziereisen winery on the way to Basel, actually ..." I purse my lips in thought.

"So, as I said, we should have left an hour ago."

"I'll get my keys." I laugh, picking up my things while Margot checks her lipstick in the mirror beside the door.

The drive south is mostly uneventful. I divide my time watching the road, the scenery, and Margot. *La Reine Margot.* Did you see the movie? Queen Margot. My queen.

Ziereisen, Krebs, Röschard. All the wineries we stop at are excellent, but I feel the car is beginning to sag rather in the rear from all my purchases. After the last stop, Margot takes the keys and drives the aptly named Baselstrasse into the city while I unsteadily fiddle with the car radio.

"Why do you drink so much?"

"I enjoy it."

"How can you even taste the wine?"

"I probably can't. Look, do we have to talk about this? I said I was sorry."

As the light changes, Margot puts the car roughly into gear and propels us forward. After a kilometre or two, I break the silence. "I am sorry. About back there."

"Could you not have any wine with lunch, please?"

I sigh and nod. "Agreed. It's hot out anyway. A bottle of water would be wise."

"Should we stop and get you a coffee?"

I shake my head. "No need."

"These are my oldest friends we're having lunch with. Please, for my sake, behave."

"I know. I'm trying."

"Then what the *hell* was that earlier?" Margot exhales, closes her eyes, gripping the steering wheel tightly as she guides the car into the Stänzlergasse, and expertly reverses into a streetside parking space. Then she turns off the ignition and removes the key.

"I don't know. I was being stupid."

"Agreed." She turns and looks at me. "Come on then."

I flip down the sun visor and look at my reflection in the small makeup mirror. "It doesn't show. Unfortunately." Margot says as she gets out of the car and shuts the driver's door after her.

It's true. The redness from her hand on my cheek had mostly disappeared. My queen. I suppose I should be grateful that lèse-majesté is no longer enforced in the courts. After too much wine, I become less than glamourous. In fact, I become a bit of a boar. The pun is intended.

I might call it wounded pride if my pride wasn't in so many tatters and hanging from so many threads that there wasn't really anything *left* to wound. Something then. A ghosting. Too many tastings previous, so at one point, I was just drinking for the raw pleasure of it. Margot was, as always, her usual, buoyant self, probably the vintner explaining things to her, was too young, too good looking, too fit, too unlike me in every respect.

"Margot, here, you have to taste this. Its fruit is almost … it's like you're biting into the stuff." I slurred, calling her to me. She turned and smiled, an embarrassed smile. So I did what any idiot would do; I marched over and tried to, playfully, mind you, coax her to sip.

She allowed me to lift the glass, and she pecked at the golden liquid, nodding and agreeing whole heartily. "Almost as if you had the soft fruit in your hand!" She exclaimed. Well, I wasn't convinced and made a show of refilling the glass and drinking it in great gulps. "How can you taste it with such a peck?" I wanted to know. And then I tried to get her to try another, larger taste.

And that is when I felt the sting of her hand.

I've never met Margot's 'Basel connection', as she calls them. Rachel and Tom are a friendly and interesting couple, but my social skills flag after the main course, and by the time the dessert plates have been cleared, I'm itching to return to the car.

As I pick up my water glass, I find my hand is shaking. Perhaps I'm in withdrawal. No. I get that sometimes. I also don't drink wine every day. There isn't a problem. We don't need to hash anything out.

Margot and her friends have their faces turned in my direction, but all I can do is smile inanely. "I'm sorry." I place my hand over Margot's. "My thoughts were elsewhere. The cake reminded me of a recipe I used to make." I can lie casually and on-demand, though it never fools Margot.

"We were thinking of going down to the river. There's a sculpture exhibition." Margot raises her eyebrows, patting my hand free.

"That sounds good." I smile, lying again. It's becoming pathologic.

Later, as we drive back towards Alsace, me at the wheel this time, Margot's silence drowns out the throaty roar of the car as it takes the twists and turns of the hilly terrain.

"I don't think this will be remembered as the best of days."

Margot breaks her silence momentarily to inhale, begins to say something, then reins it in again before turning and looking out the window as the vineyards fade away in the summer twilight.

"Would you mind if we went home earlier?"

I've done it this time. I've upset her terribly, but I can't let on. My pride, you understand. I must pretend I don't know what's going on. That's my usual response to things.

"Of course. We'll miss going to Riquewihr though. Is everything okay? We can head back tomorrow if you like." I chuckle in a way that I know she dislikes but honestly, we can be honest with each other; I hope, honestly, I have no control over it. It's just how I laugh at these moments. I have heard it described as a 'sarcastic laugh', but I don't mean it to be. "The car is probably carrying as much wine as it will hold anyway. We're full. Time to head back."

"Yes. I want to go home because of the wine." Margot says, then continues her vigil at the passenger seat. My poor queen. I am such a fool.

margaret

Annie and I are biding our time outside the coffee shop, undecided on whether to cross to the next section of the park or head back.

"What do you think, girl?" I eye the coffee shop with great desire. Two lemons and three persimmons weigh down the plastic bag in my left hand; Annie's leash in my right. There are no extra hands in which to hold a coffee. I would have gone to the market on the way home, but they were closing as we passed.

"Shall we risk getting a coffee?" Annie barks her agreement, so we go inside. I transfer the bag of fruit and the leash to my left hand, wait for the person in front of me to get their coffee, then order mine.

"Medium cappuccino to go, please. Umm, a bit less milk? Thanks." The barista asks for my name. "Mike." I casually lie. Annie barks her disapproval. I look down and shrug. "Data privacy. It's a human thing."

Annie barks again, loudly, looking behind me. I turn to see Margaret. "Hello, you two."

"Hey, you."

We kiss, and Margaret ruffles Annie's head. "What brings you out? We were just going to head over to the other half of the park."

"I'll join you. I can't get my head around work at the moment, so I decided to see if I could catch up with you."

"Cappucino for Mike?" The barista calls, and I walk over and take my cup sheepishly.

"Umm, you could take the fruit, actually. Or Annie?"

"Mike?" Margaret laughs. "Who's he?"

Annie barks. "Okay, you two. It's my stage name. Well, coffee name to be precise."

"You have other names?" Margaret looks down at Annie. "Who's the funny man, eh Annie?"

"Haha, you two." I pass the leash to Margaret. "Here. Thanks."

We leave the shop and walk in the direction of the park's south half on the other side of the river.

"I hope Mike doesn't come into general use. I don't want us to be known as M&M." Margaret reaches over for my coffee with her free hand.

"I'm sorry. I didn't ask if you wanted one."

She shakes her head. "No worries, I don't. Just a sip." She takes a sip of my cappuccino and hands back the cup. "Thanks. I was curious what kind of coffee Mike drinks."

"Do *you* use your real name at coffee shops?"

"Probably. I don't *think* I use an alias."

"It's *not* an alias."

"My boyfriend, the gangster." Margaret chuckles.

"The love bandit." I riposte.

"Hahaha!" Margaret laughs deeply. "Okay, you win." She shakes her head, smiling, "Love bandit. Heh heh."

"Has Annie been good?"

"Golden."

Margaret looks down at Annie, gently pulling the leash. "Has Mike been a good boy, Annie? Did you have a nice time in the park?"

Annie barks and hops about happily.

We walk to the end of the street and turn into the park, connected by a long wooden bridge crossing a narrow stream.

"Meaghan," I say without preamble.

"Who's Meaghan?" Margaret turns to me.

"Your alias. Your coffee name."

"Meaghan? *That's* your choice?" She laughs.

"My first guess was Millicent, but I went with Meaghan after a little consideration."

"Oh boy. Keep on considering. Meaghan." Margaret shakes her head.

Crossing the bridge, we come to a fork in the path. "Right or left?" I ask.

"Let's let Annie decide." Margaret lets the leash go limp. Annie looks both ways, panting slightly. Then she barks and moves to the right, so we follow.

"Good choice, Annie; you know your way around. The leash-free area is this way."

"Susan," Margaret says.

"Who's Susan?"

"She's your Mike. They even sound like a couple."

"Your coffee name is Susan? Then we'll be known as S&M!" I laugh.

"Haha! No, my actual name is Susan."

I stop, looking at her as she continues a few paces further before turning around.

"Your middle initial stands for Susan?"

"Yes."

"You never told me that."

"You never asked."

"I never *stopped* asking."

She shrugs and continues walking, and I trot to catch up. "I like it. Susan."

"Oh, good. I can keep it then?"

"You're funny. Susan. I do like it. Though …"

"What?"

"I always thought your middle initial stood for Sybille."

"Sybille?!" Margaret frowns, looking at me. "Meaghan, Millicent, Sybille ... is that how you see me? A character in some romantic novel?" She laughs and comments to Annie. "What a silly man he is, isn't he, Annie?"

Annie barks happily.

"Two against one. Very fair. A typical Susan tactic."

Margaret continues laughing as we come to the leash-free area of the park. She bends down, gives Annie a rub, and removes her leash. Annie runs happily off, and Margaret pushes herself against me with a kiss.

Annie and the other dogs scamper playfully together in the enclosed leash-free area as Margaret, and I find an unoccupied bench. We recognize a few people and raise our hands in greeting to those we've talked with in the past.

Dogs are a bond. You don't get too many cat people here. A lot of horse people, though.

"Where do they even keep their horses?"

"Probably out past the suburbs."

"Seems expensive."

"There's a luxury tax on horses."

"Ironic. They've definitely made a comeback."

"How do you mean?"

"Well, the rich had horses, then everyone had them, and now it's the rich again."

"Everybody had a horse?"

I nod. "In the same way that everybody now has a car. Of course, not exactly in the same way, but …."

Margaret chuckles. "I get your point."

We sit back and, in various stages, entangle our fingers our hands; finally, my arm is around Margaret's shoulder, and she is leaning against me. This is a good moment, I think. As good a reason as any to ruin it.

"You remember me telling you about the articles I was writing for the FinTech company?"

"Hmm, not specifically. You tell me about a lot of tech articles. They all sound the same to me. Sorry. It's really not my line."

I nod and smile, squeezing her shoulder gently. "No, no problem. Yes, the articles are a real mixed bag, but all somehow tech-related, you're right. These were the articles about FinTech lead generation for those guys back east."

Margaret giggles. We've moved from chuckling to giggling, so she's in a good mood. "Guys back east? Sounds interesting. Is this why you brought me to a bench in the middle of the park? To talk about work you do for guys back east? Does this have anything to do with your alias? Do you want to check me for a wire before you say anything else?" Margaret breaks into laughter. "I'm sorry."

"Haha, yes, very droll. So, I've been writing these articles for those guys who do that stuff, you know? Yes. So they asked if I'd be interested in doing it full-time. Back East. In New York."

Margaret sits up, untangling herself from my arm. "Really? That sounds interesting."

I nod, finishing the coffee in my cup, looking out as Annie runs fast across the field chasing another dog. "What do you think?"

"I think it's a great opportunity. Wow. That's what you always wanted to do, write full time."

My nodding quickens. "True, but I don't know if I want to live in New York, and … and more importantly there is us."

"I can't move to New York. I have my teaching here."

"I know."

Margaret waves as Annie runs towards us. "It's a four-hour flight."

"At least."

"When did they ask you?"

"Last week."

"Last week?"

"I'm not going to consider it if you can't go."

"I can't go. Not like this. I mean, so fast. When do they want you to start?"

"Next month?"

"Wow. That is fast."

"Then I'll tell them no."

"Wait. You might not get another chance like this again."

"I won't get another chance like us again either."

marjorie

The taxi ride from the shopping mall to the hotel was uneventful. Marjorie hadn't been waiting long as she texted me her position at the same time that I rose out of the metro station across from the busy intersection. A stroke of luck.

"Hi!" She waved from across the street.

"Wait there!" I looked for traffic then ran across to her. "Hi."

Marjorie smiles, putting her phone back into her purse. "I just got here."

"Good. Shall we take a taxi to the hotel, or shall we walk?"

She considers this for a moment. "Taxi?"

I nod. "Sounds good. The hotel is that way, and on a warmer day, it would be a nice walk." I point into the distance across the lagoon, resplendent with a fountain and tour boats. "As it is, a taxi is probably better."

Marjorie nods. "We just need to find one."

"Indeed. As you say, we just need to find one."

Taxis are as notoriously omnipresent as pigeons in any major city until you need one. "There's a taxi rank behind that building. I point, and we begin walking. "At least there used to be." I chuckle.

We found a taxi rather painlessly ten minutes later and found a cosy table in the hotel restaurant without any difficulty.

"I thought it would be busier. I even considered reserving." We look around the half-empty space. "Lucky."

By the time we are halfway through our lunches, the restaurant is full, and we are feeling quite smug about arriving when we did.

Marjorie's pasta plate empties itself slowly while I try to pace myself with her. I eat too quickly; she eats too slowly. That's not really true. She eats properly. She discovers and smells, tastes and enjoys, chews and considers her food. In earlier times, we might have said she eats like a lady, which isn't a bad way to eat even today. Our stomachs having no teeth, I mean.

"You're not having any wine with lunch?"

I shake my head. "Water is fine. I'm keeping pace with you."

She raises her eyebrows. "Is that a good thing?"

"You're a very good example."

Marjorie blushes. "You have me on some sort of pedestal." She laughs. "You know I'm a very bad example in many ways."

I nod and take a sip of water. "True." I smile. "In many ways, however, you are a very good example."

She sits back. "Whoa. I'm stuffed. That was delicious."

I nod. "It was. Good choice. I'm glad I followed your suggestion."

Marjorie laughs. "I didn't suggest a thing. I ordered, and you took the same."

I raise an eyebrow. "I followed your lead then."

"Hmm. So how am I a good example?"

"Oh, many ways. You're mindful and caring. You eat well. You don't use stimulants or opiates. You aren't involved in any organised crime …."

Marjorie laughs. "Opiates? You could say the same of most people. Organised crime … you're a nut."

"You are a considerate and good person. At another time, you would be a wise woman. Some sort of healer or teacher."

"Oh, Jesus. I'm off for some cake. You should order a scotch. One meal without alcohol, and you're off your head." She reaches out and places her hand on mine. "You're sweet. Order me a coffee, please?" I nod. She gets up, laughing, and walks to the cake counter at the far end of the restaurant.

I watch her go. This is my favourite part of the day. Well, I don't yet know that it's been the favourite part of my day. Later it will become clear that this was, in fact, the moment that I don't forget.

She walks away from our table and moves somewhat unsteadily through the forest of other tables scattered about the dining room. Time sort of slows down as she moves, and I think, you know, I could certainly fall in love with her from this angle, how she uses her hands and arms to balance herself ever so slightly as she walks. Then she reaches the selection of cakes and peruses the selection, lost in her thoughts. She looks back and smiles at me, and I fall in love with her all over again.

As she returns, I look down at my phone and look up just before she regains her seat. "Did you find anything?"

She shakes her head. "Yes, but I'll pass. Just the coffee."

I nod. "The waitress hasn't been by yet." And, of course, at that moment, she arrives at my elbow.

We both order coffee, without any cake. "Pacing yourself again?" Marjorie laughs.

I smile. "No. I had everything I needed watching you."

Marjorie rolls her eyes. "The last of the big-time charmers."

Our coffees arrive. Marjorie stirs hers with a studied turn of the wrist.

"It's weird, yeah. I get it, but I really like watching you. You walk in a very focused way."

"It's called not wanting to fall."

"Haha. Come on then, drink up and let's think about catching that train back."

Not having any dessert meant I pause in front of the doughnut shop in the train station but did not go in. My excuse was the old typewriter sitting in the window next to a pair of battered suitcases. I can understand the latter props, but why anyone would be lugging an old typewriter about on their travels these days were lost on me. Perhaps the connection to storytelling and travel? The travelling journalist or war reporter? It looked at least a hundred years old, and many of the keys were missing.

It reminded me that I have always wanted to take my portable typewriter to a coffee shop. While everyone tapped quietly away on their laptops, I would assure myself with the clean strokes of my Olivetti Traveller Deluxe. However, I'm made of too timid stuff.

I love typewriters and wish I had more space to give in to my passion. I also wish I had a turntable so I could spend Saturday mornings browsing the flea markets for old LPs. It wasn't even an excuse to stop but the reason.

Majorie is waiting.

"Are you coming? We'll miss our train."

"Sorry!" I run over to her. "Did you see the old typewriter in the window?"

"Why would they have an old typewriter in the window?"

"I was asking myself the very same question."

"Do you want water for the trip?"

Marjorie is eyeing the bottled water recklessly stacked in a pyramid outside the delicatessen. "Good idea." I nod as she takes two bottles from the top. I flinch inwardly, expecting the display to topple, but it doesn't even whimper.

"Let's go."

Marjorie passes me a bottle, stuffing the other into the depths of her town coat, and we scamper up the stairway to the platform. However, it doesn't appear to be the platform for the trains going in our direction, so we go back down and up the other side just as our train arrives.

"That was lucky."

"Yes. I wouldn't have liked to have waited for the next one."

The whistle blows shortly after we gain our seats, the train car jostles, and we fall into their dusty comfort with a laugh.

margarida

I stuff the four bags of newspaper and clay into the garbage bins at the back of the building. Well, not exactly. I was able to get the small remnants of clay past Margarida; there was no way I was separating every morsel from the paper, and the pieces remaining were small. I did have to shake the paper out of the plastic bags and place those into their respective recycling bins. Margarida is a stickler for recycling, but I'm not convinced. Love blooms in the strangest of places.

We walk hand in hand down the hill towards the main street, rich with lights and signs. It feels odd holding hands. Have you ever felt that? When I was very young, it felt odd too. Nice, but odd. I don't think I've ever gotten over that feeling. However, it's not something you see every day. People holding hands? I always notice, and I think because it's so rare. And it's sort of unnatural too. It doesn't serve any function and probably gets in the way if you suddenly need that hand. It's also tricky to get your hand back. After you've scratched your nose or rubbed your eye or whatever you need to do with your hand at that moment, you can't give it back again. The moment is broken.

But I digress. We walk hand in hand down the hill towards the main street. After passing a few bistros, Margarida retrieves her hand from mine to sneeze.

"Achoo!" She sneezes, covering her mouth. "Sorry." Then she holds out her hand for me to take, and because I love her, I take it without comment. It's a bit like her habit of spearing pieces of food from my plate or sharing a large portion of fish and chips. Call me twisted and wrong, but I find something very sensual about this closeness.

She points across the street. "How about Mikos?" We slow down, then stop. Considering the small restaurant across from us. We've often passed but never entered.

We consider in silence for a moment.

"We could. Why have we never eaten there?"

Margarida raises her eyebrows. "I don't know."

"It sounds Japanese but looks Greek."

"Fried squid or raw squid?"

"I prefer fried."

"Shall we try it?" She gently pulls my hand as she takes a step toward the curb.

"Okay. I consider a moment longer. Let's try."

We look, then dash across the street in the few seconds which are free of traffic. There is no lineup outside the restaurant. Peering in the windows, it appears half full. "Half full is good."

I nod and open the door, holding it for her.

We order a smaller than expected dinner and drink a larger than expected carafe of wine. We order a second carafe which is unusual for us, but Margarida is in a celebratory mood, and I never say no to more wine. Mostly never.

We shared a delicious Fettuccini Alfredo to start, a dish we both love but are never able to finish a portion. So rich. After that, a salad of green tomatoes, onions, and fish for the main course. Grilled swordfish, moist and salty.

About halfway through the fish, I sit back to take a breather. "I'm stuffed. I should have ordered a lighter fish."

Margarida laughs. "You're never able to finish a meal."

"I don't know where you put it all. You're so tiny." I help myself to some more wine and pour some into Margarida's glass. "You haven't told me what the library plan to do with the pots."

She takes a large mouthful of wine, her face pleasantly flushed, and leans forward. "It seems that their next focus is Portugal and Spain, their history, food, drink – the entire cultural pallet. There's an annual Amphora Day in Portugal apparently, on St. Martin's Day, and long story short, they want me to make some. A lot."

She sits back, proud of herself, as am I, and empties her glass.

"Amphora?" I raise my eyebrows and refill her glass. "Those look trickier than pots. Have you ever made one?"

Margarida shakes her head. "Never."

"Uh-huh."

"But don't you see? That's why it's so exciting. I love trying out new things."

I nod. "Yes. Wow. I'm impressed. It sounds interesting. How many do you need to make?"

"As many as possible, probably. They said they would like to have a wall of them. You know the glass inside the wall?"

"That's a long indoor wall. Window." I nod.

"Well, it won't be the entire wall, thank goodness. Probably just one end. You know how they have a feature in each section as you walk along?"

I continue to nod. "How much are they paying?"

Margarida makes a face. "Not very much. Materials and an artist's fee."

"How much is that?"

"Five hundred dollars."

I inhale deeply. "Wow. That isn't very much, is it?"

Margarida shakes her head. "No. Though I'm just editing my book now, if I get three amphorae done a day, I imagine it's all done in ten days. It's a good way to get my name out."

"Amphorae?"

"The plural of amphora."

"Really? The things you know."

She laughs, reaching over to take my hand and leaning forward to kiss me. I lean forward and kiss her. She's so happy. "That's why you love me, isn't it? My vast knowledge?"

I chuckle. "For no other reason. My lovely encyclopedia."

We sip our wine as the waiter clears our plates. I visualize the interior window running along the library facing the mall. Thirty amphorae won't make a dent in even one of those sections.

"Are you sure thirty will be enough?"

"I hope so." She sits back, slowly releasing my hand. "Will you help?"

"Me? I don't know the first thing about pottery; you know that."

"You could help me paint them."

"They need to be painted?"

Margarida nods, making a pained expression, and drinks the remainder of her wine.

"We don't have to glaze them and fill them with wine, too, do we?"

Margarida laughs. "I was saving that news for later."

I laugh and reach out for her hand. "I love you. It's been a wonderful year."

"It has. Thank you for a lovely dinner." Margarida nods.

"Would you like some dessert?" I nod towards the dessert trolley on the other side of the room.

Margarida looks at me with a raised eyebrow and a tipsy twinkle in her eye. "Oh, I want dessert, but back at my place." She winks. "Would that be an idea?"

"Your place is almost too far away. Check, please!" I laugh.

margarethe

Dinner was so delicious I can still taste it. The creamy richness of the sauce, the peppery undertones of the mushrooms, the lightness of the risotto, the subtle top notes of the wine and cheese … well, you just had to be there. I'm glad you weren't. I'm glad to have only shared that meal with Margarethe.

After dessert, we necked like teenagers on the couch until Margarethe shooed me away. Fair enough. We both have early morning appointments, and when we make love, we are up all night touching each other gently in the darkness. It's exquisite.

I turn to look at my clock, which will ring in ten minutes. I always feel cheated out of the five or ten minutes prior to the alarm that I invariably wake.

I walk to the kitchen, pour a glass of water from the tap after letting it run first, and pick up my phone from the desk where it charges overnight.

Have you ever drunk water straight from the tap after it's been sitting in the pipes all night? Then you know how horrible it tastes. And no, you shouldn't sleep with your phone in the bedroom. If you're meant to hear the ring, you will.

Hey, you. Hi. Good morning. Last night was wonderful. So delicious! As was the risotto. Thank you.

I follow that up with a series of emojis oft sent through the ether between us, little confirmations that we are still teenagers at heart.

What is *your* morning regimen like? I push up and sit up, take my vitamins and my heart medication, drink a coffee, eat some yoghurt with a mixture of what I hope are healthy grains, seeds and flakes I mix myself. None of them come in a colourful package, so they must be healthy.

Were you expecting an Egg McMuffin? I do come across as a tad unhealthy, don't I? I would kill for an Egg McMuffin if the truth were told, but I'm trying to live long enough to live with Margarethe and have a few years together. I want a year or two of just us. I really only have that on my bucket list.

While the coffee machine is warming, I shower, check my emails, and then find the location of my meeting on Google Maps.

I don't have any notifications set on my phone, which means I'm always looking at it to see if something has come in. Oddly enough, I'm only on my phone for two hours and seven minutes a day on average. I was surprised too. That's fifteen per cent less time than a week ago too.

It was good. I miss you. Call me after your meeting? I'll be out of my meeting by noon. xxx

I hesitate, but don't give in to the urge to add 'I love you'. I'm trying to say it less, make it special. It's like being in AA. Or on a diet. This constant temptation.

Margarethe says it sparingly. She hardly says 'I love you' at all, but when she does, I feel amazing. Surprised almost, like it's the first time she's ever said it. It's like a gift, unexpectedly received.

That's the effect I want to have on her, but it's not going to happen if I say 'I love you' with the same frequency as I ask, 'how was your day?' As twisted as it may seem, if you say 'I love you' every day, the magic simply wears out. It's a pain because it's the only thing I can think of that expresses how I feel. Our language is so limited; it's really only physically that we can express exactly how we feel.

You're offended. I can tell, and I would be too. Here is a couple with everything so perfectly wrapped up and polished that their biggest problem is saying 'I love you' too often. Nauseating, isn't it?

That's my fault because I was led to the first-world problem of the relationship by our texting this morning. The real problem is me. I don't listen. Probably a problem for most men. It is. I just Googled it. Why Men Don't Listen: 10 Reasons and How To Deal with Them. According to

Psychology Today ... well, that's enough to validate your problem, seeing it discussed in Psychology Today.

After my meeting, I stop by the florist and buy four bunches of tulips. When it comes to flowers, bigger really *is* better. Remember the scene in Charles' room the morning after Sebastian vomited through his open window? Something along the lines of 'my room was filled with what appeared to be and turned out was the entire stock of a flower stall'. Along those lines. Unless plucked from the middle of the Gobi Desert or atop Mount Everest, a single flower seems niggardly.

Margarethe and I have agreed to meet for coffee before heading back to our separate abodes later in the afternoon. She has a regular schedule of various online meetings and classes, as do I. Sharing a place would be a logistical challenge if only when talking about office space and internet speed. Would we be talking about three bedrooms? When you're alone, the home office and living room work well together, but as a couple, perhaps not. There has to be a place of nonwork to which you can both retreat.

I push myself into the café with my embarrassing armful of tulips just as Margarethe turns around from placing her coat on the back of the chair. People look up and smile, but Margarethe's laugh is worth more than the price of the flowers.

"Oh my god." She covers her face and giggles. "What are all these?"

I move them to the side as I lean in for a kiss. "They're tulips." I laugh, pleased by my explanation as though I've just discovered some unknown fossil. "Aren't they beautiful?"

"They are. Thank you." Margarethe takes them in her arms, turning helplessly for a moment until a very nice waitress comes over with a bucket and places it on one of the unoccupied chairs at our table. Margarethe laughs. "Thank you!"

"You're welcome. Can I bring you something to drink?"

"A decaffeinated latte macchiato please?"

"Cappucino, please. Fully caffeinated."

The waitress smiles and nods, turning back to the counter.

"What did I do to deserve this … grandiose display of affection?"

We sit down beside each other, joining hands on top of the table. "Nothing. Just … nothing. An expression of my pleasure at the thought of seeing you?"

"You're taking them away then, now that you've seen me?" Margarethe laughs.

"Oh no." I chuckle. "You're stuck with them. I'll drive you back home, so you don't have to carry them on the bus."

"Thank you." She squeezes my hand and sits back with a content and happy smile.

"I got a little carried away. A few tulips didn't feel right."

"You're amazing."

"You are."

"We could keep this up all day."

"Or all night."

"Friday night?"

"I can't wait."

Our coffee arrives, and we sit back in our chairs, breaking the spell for a moment as the waitress asks about cake.

Margarethe shakes her head. "I have my weight to watch. Remember?"

I laugh. "As long as I don't have to carry you while jogging, I think you're good." I look up at the waitress. "A piece of your buckwheat meringue, please. Two forks?"

"How was your day? How did your meeting go?"

"It went well, thank you. And yours?"

"Blessedly short. You know me. I hate meetings. Talking about things. Just do them, I say."

"If you don't talk about them, then how would you know what to do."

"I think most of the time how you do things is inherent in what it is you want to do."

"Sounds profound."

"It's lost on most people."

"I see why you freelance."

"My team-playing skills? Or lack thereof to be precise." I laugh.

Margarethe winks, and our cake arrives. "I'm glad you got two forks. I think I will have a bite."

margriet

Even as the moving men unload the truck, we're agreed but still undecided. Anything labelled 'office' goes into the room on the left, anything labelled 'bedroom' to the right. The rest of the boxes are easy to sort, so we only stuck up the two signs. Bedroom. Office.

Margriet and I leave the men to their work, only once having to unwrap something after it hits the floor.

"We aren't in a rush. Please take your time." She had politely admonished. But only once.

They had picked up at my place first, which meant Margriet's boxes were coming in first. There were more of them than mine. Many more.

While she had been in the same place for many years and collected many books, files, folios, and other teaching and research paraphernalia, I had moved about frequently. Most of my books had disappeared. I now had a very small collection. I could be sexist and say, of course, she had more clothes and shoes, but it was simply a fact. She outweighed me in closet and drawer space three to one.

As the boxes in the bedroom and the office, as they were currently labelled, increased, we were still undecided.

This will be our final home, and it will be a home together. We had spent days, weekends, weeks, and the occasional month together, always with the understanding that another place, our own place, existed and could be retreated to at some point in time.

Now there was to be no retreat. We were in it together until the end.

We would continue to work, so an office was a must. We would also continue to sleep, make love, and be sick, so a bedroom was a requirement too.

"I'm glad we finally decided to move in together," I say, walking into the kitchen where Margriet is unwrapping glasses. Moving day is a lot like Christmas, unwrapping things you forgot you packed like so many presents.

"Me too. I was about to give up on you."

"What do you mean? I thought you were happy living alone."

"I was. I could have stayed living alone. I didn't think you'd ever decide to move in together. It's going to be nicer not to be alone as we get older. Don't you think?"

"We'll be getting crotchety. It might be rough, being grumpy together." I laugh.

Margriet unwraps another glass, placing it carefully in the cupboard. "I think we're already there." She laughs. "We know each other well enough, and we've seen each other's dark sides."

I raise an eyebrow. "Dark side? Now that sounds interesting, Frau Doctor."

Margriet slaps me away as I walk towards her with a leering grin. "Go make yourself useful. Make sure the van is emptied."

"Okay, okay." I laugh, raising my hands in defeat.

As I walk down the hallway towards the door, she calls, "Don't let them drive away with my jewels!"

At that moment, two movers enter and look at me questioningly.

"Paste. All her jewels are in a safe deposit box." I wink.

I walk downstairs and make a slow tour of the driveway, the green area between the apartment building and the street, the garbage bins discreetly housed behind tastefully landscaped walls of stone and ivy. It's not the area I would have chosen, but vacant living space is scarce. We were lucky to get this place.

I make my way back up from the moving van after cajoling one of the movers into letting me carry a box. "We're not insured for that."

"I take full responsibility."

He didn't seem convinced but was too tired to care. Poor chap.

Back upstairs, Margriet is dragging a box of books down the hallway from the living room to the room marked 'Office'.

"Does that large room look like the office?"

"Maybe they're used to moving businesses rather than homes." I venture.

She stands up, holding her waist between her hands, her face slightly red. "These books weigh a ton."

I laugh. "That's why we got movers."

I place the box I am carrying on the bedroom floor as Margriet walks in.

"What are you thinking?"

"About the bedroom and office." I walk over to the window and admire the view. "Nice view."

"Are you worried about sleeping with me each night now?"

I smile. "I love the thought of holding you each night."

"We won't be having sex every night." Margriet laughs.

I pretend to look crestfallen. "What? This is news to me."

She rolls her eyes. "It's all you think about."

"That's your fault. Just look at you. You're an object of desire." I chuckle.

Margriet raises an eyebrow.

"Vision. A vision of desire."

She shakes her head and laughs.

"Do you want to each have a bedroom and put desks in the living room?"

"No. Definitely not that. I want a work-free living space."

Margriet nods. "So do I."

"Which means a desk in each bedroom." I look at her. "If that's what we're talking about."

"*Is* that what we're talking about?"

I pause and breathe in and out deeply, slowly, not knowing what to answer. "Part of me wants to say yes; most of me wants to say no."

Margriet nods. "We talked about this before. Think about it before they bring the furniture up."

She walks out, and I follow. "We only have the one bed." Margriet walks into the living room and admires the growing stack of boxes. "And the one desk." She turns to me. "You sold yours."

"I don't need them. Didn't think I needed them." We look at each other. "Don't."

Margriet shrugs and walks back into the kitchen, and I follow her. "Why are we talking about this again now?"

"I don't know. You brought it up. You must have some thoughts."

"*I* brought it up?"

"Okay, I did. I may be worried."

"You're always worried about something. I'm not worried."

"Okay then. We'll have the one office and the one bedroom like we planned." I laugh. "We can always move furniture around later." I nod. "We may fight, and not want to sleep with each other."

Margriet snorts. "If we fight you can sleep on the floor." She lifts another box to the table and opens the flaps. "You can always sleep on the couch in the living room if you change your mind about sleeping with me." She unwraps another glass and places it on the table. "I'm not moving any furniture."

margisia

"Are you angry?"

"No."

"You seem angry."

"I'm not."

"I'm sorry."

"It's not important. Let's forget about it."

"Okay."

There is a hesitancy in our voices this morning. At some point last night, I broke the tenderness of the moment. Some comment. I'm not going to repeat it here. I thought I was being charming, but only those dapper fellows in old movies can carry that off. I tend to forget the women are actresses and paid not to slap any faces. If I'm not often a swine, I'm often a bull in a china shop.

"Let me start on a good footing and bring you some tea." I place my hand on her bare shoulder and climb out of bed.

"It's really okay. But I won't say no to a cup of tea."

We smile at each other; then I walk to the kitchen.

"Put on some shorts!" Her voice beneath the comforter is muffled as I gain the hallway. "The neighbours might be out."

Good point. I walk back into the bedroom and scan the floor for my boxers, finding them beside her panties near the foot of the bed. Pulling them on, I also grab a t-shirt and finish getting dressed as I walk down the hallway toward the kitchen.

The neighbours are indeed up, standing on their balcony, each enjoying a morning cigarette and coffee. I return their greeting with a wave as I fill the kettle with water. Margisia's balcony is fortunate enough to have an unobscured view of the street. Outside, her kitchen window was once free, but a new block of flats rose last year. At least the people across the way are friendly and quiet.

I prepare two cups of Earl Grey, place a few ginger snaps on the saucer of each cup, and carry them into the bedroom.

"Here you are." I hand Margisia a cup.

"Cookies? Trying to sweeten me up?"

I sit on the bed beside her. "But you're already so sweet."

She rolls her eyes, looks at me, and sips her tea. "Thank you."

"About last night."

"Please, forget it."

"No, it was thoughtless. I was going for charming, but I somehow landed on obnoxious."

"You don't need to charm me. We're here together. Whenever you mention a past girlfriend, I feel like you aren't present. That you're thinking about her instead of me."

I nod my head. "I know. I wasn't. I was trying to compliment you. It was stupid, and I'm sorry."

"The best compliment you can give me is to be mindful of us. There is only us. Be present, here, with us."

"And again, you are right." I nod. I feel stupid.

Margisia laughs. "You're such a little boy. That can be charming in itself, but only in very small doses. Very small." She winks and reaches out her hand to stroke my face.

"Okay. Sorry. Thanks." I lean over, and we kiss. Margisia has the most beautiful, plump, naturally red lips. I could kiss her all day long. There you see it too. I'm just a little boy in a man's body.

"Mm, you smell good."

"So do you."

Our kisses lengthen, deepen, and we fall back into the bed after depositing our cups on the small table beside the bed. "I …"

Margisia presses a finger against my lips, pushing herself against me. "Shut up."

Our lovemaking is gentle and slow as always. Caring. Sensual. Even as our movements increase in tempo, our lips are grazing each other, tongues flicking lightly and playfully, our eyes staring and watching the other. She smells so good. Feels so good. I want this moment to continue forever.

We wake up after an hour, or is it longer? Tangled in the sheets, wrapped in each other's arms, the stickiness drying on our thighs and stomachs.

"Hey." Margisia smiles, and we kiss, our faces centimetres apart.

"Hey."

She closes her eyes and burrows closer against me.

The telephone ringing in the kitchen wakes us up again, this time much later.

"Oh!" Margisia sits up, looks over at her clock and laughs. "Oh my God, it's noon!"

I laugh. "You know how I hate oversleeping."

I get out of bed and walk quickly into the kitchen, picking up her phone and bringing it into the bedroom. "Do you want to answer it?"

Margisia shakes her head, so I place it on the dresser and go in search of my own phone. Finding it in the living room, I see there are messages but no calls. I walk back into the bedroom and fall onto the bed. "You were incredible."

"I know." Margisia smiles, climbing into her pyjamas before walking out of the bedroom. "I'm going to shower. Make me a coffee please?"

"Sure." I get up and follow her. "I was pretty good too, right?"

Margisia laughs and pulls the bathroom door behind her. "Pretty good, yes."

I laugh and walk into the kitchen as the sound of the shower and her singing come from the half-closed bathroom door.

"Pretty good?" I frown. "I thought I was more than pretty good." I chuckle.

It's a rare day that we don't need to be somewhere or face a deadline, a class, a meeting, something online that needs to be done. Today is one of those rarities.

I prepare two coffees, take them into the bathroom, opening the door to a wall of steam. "Shall I open the window?" I place one of the coffees on the counter.

"I don't know. Do you want me to hurt you?"

I laugh. "Okay, okay. I was just worried about the paint peeling off the walls."

The shower turns off, and Margisia steps out; taking the towel, I hand her. Her long black hair clings to her shoulders and her breasts. Undressed, she appears very small. "See? The water was so hot you shrank."

She sticks out her tongue and pads over to the counter for her coffee. "Beast." She sips the coffee, closing her eyes in pleasure. "Mmm. Thank you."

"Are you finished? I'll have a shower if you are."

She nods, and I step into the stall, closing the glass doors behind me.

"Do you have anything planned for today?"

"Not a thing."

"Want to go to the museum?"

"That would be a great idea. Yes. We can walk in the park too."

"Sounds good."

I let the hot water pour over me, closing my eyes as the stream washes away the previous hours, and smile, very happy, thinking about the day we have together and how rare and wonderful that is.

marjatta

Long before Marjatta and I moved into our house, I saw her there. When I say house, I mean cottage. I guess it's the same. I just don't want you to be disappointed. It's also very near the river and on the wrong side of the dike. How you possibly imagined I could have afforded more, I don't know. This may be fiction, but it's not fantasy fiction.

As I walked down the street and turned into the gravel drive, I always saw Marjatta on her knees at the front of the house, tending the flower bed. The rustle of the stones beneath my shoes caused her to turn her head, and she would smile, brushing the hair out of her face with a gloved hand.

When the house was unexpectedly put up for sale, I bought it. Marjatta planted flowers in the front and herbs in the back, and I mowed the lawn in the summer and raked leaves in the autumn. Just as I had imagined it.

Today, as I return from the shops with the newspaper and milk, Marjatta is already busy on the front porch, crushing the seashells she collected on our trip and brought home. "Good for the plants." She says.

I know absolutely nothing about shells, imagining them to be the work of years of natural labour. Marjatta is much smarter than I am. A wise woman in every sense of the word.

"Count the rings." She held up one of the shells she had picked up, turning it in the sunlight until we made out the rings.

"Like a tree? I never knew that."

She laughed. "There is so much you don't know." She leaned over and kissed me.

"Do I get a kiss for everything I don't know? I can think of a hundred things I don't know about the seaside alone. For example, where does sand come from?" I wave my hand before me, taking in the expanse of golden sand marked with our footprints stretching away back to our hotel.

"One kiss a question a day." She laughed. "Concentrate on the shell."

I frown playfully and take her hand in mine, holding it steady. "Hmm." I squint and count the rings. "About thirty? Do you think?"

Marjatta nods. "Sounds close enough."

"So the shell is thirty years old?" She lowers her hand and places the shell in the string bag she brought for her task.

"You're going to crush the poor shell? It took thirty years to grow, then it had to make its way up to the shore, and you're just going to grind it to dust for your flower garden?" I shake my head. "It seems harsh. Quite unlike you."

"It's not years, Darling; it's days. Each ring is about a day."

"A day?! Wow. A shell grows fast. I would have guessed it took years."

"You're thinking of rocks. And trees."

I nod. "Hmm."

"So, what, the shells have calcium? Salt? Is it like crushing eggshells and mixing them with the dirt? A friend of mine did that. Years ago"

Marjatta nods. "They add nutrients, help with the PH balance, and they stop the soil compacting, so more air and water get to the roots."

I nod and follow slowly behind her as she chooses some more.

"So then tell me, please, why do so many people decorate their *bathrooms* with shells?"

Marjatta laughs heartily. "I'm sorry, but you don't get a kiss for that one – even *I* don't know the answer!"

"I've got milk." I proudly hold the paper bag in my hand like a trophy. "Would you like a coffee?"

Marjatta looks up and nods. "Please. I'll be in shortly."

"Don't rush. I'll bring it outside."

She goes back to her digging, and I go into the kitchen, remove the milk from the paper bag, and prepare the coffee percolator. From within the newspaper, I remove the letter I had retrieved from the mailbox at the gate, tearing it open with shaking hands.

After reading it, I fold the letter and the envelope together, tear them in half and push them deep into the recycling box with the rest of the paper trash.

The sounds and aroma of coffee remind me that the percolator is done, its metal base rocking like an agitated dancer on the hot plate. I place the small copper pot of milk on the still hot surface and turn the heat down to low.

I take the two cups of coffee outside, placing them on the small metal table near the porch, flanked by two white metal chairs rarely used. Marjatta stands up and comes over, removing her gloves and wiping the back of her hand across her forehead. "Thank you." She smiles, placing her hand on my arm. "Was there any mail today?"

I shake my head. "Nothing."

She picks up her coffee and inhales the steam before drinking. "Mmm smells good. Thank you."

I watch her and smile, still so in love.

"I can see you." She laughs.

"I hope so." I return the chuckle. She still doesn't like me admiring her, even after all these years.

"You should call Dr Yates. It's odd that there's still been no letter about the results."

I take a mouthful of my coffee. "I will. I'm sure it will arrive soon. It's a busy time for the labs. They have other priorities."

"Still."

"I'll call tomorrow."

"Why wait?"

You, of all women, who know me better than I know myself ask me why I am waiting? I'm sure you already know the test results were positive, and now you are dancing about in your irresistibly girlish way until I give in and tell you. I love you and your ways, and I will miss them horribly.

We should have started earlier. Ironically, I didn't want to settle down with you because it meant the end. It meant that I knew how the story would end, which is the death knell for us writers. Knowing the ending. No author wants to know the ending. because as soon as it becomes clear, gut-wrenching emptiness wells up inside, only be overcome with the arrival of a new book idea. A fresh beginning.

It's the story, the inexplicable not knowing, that keeps us alive. And by us, I mean me.

We purveyors of fiction live for our experiences and the steady stream of endless possibilities that lay before us. We aren't historians. We are dreamers. We live in possible worlds, not those already trodden.

"Du?" Marjatta returns to her native German at times of tenderness. And anger.

She pushes gently against my arm, looking up at me.

"Hmm?" I smile and gently, playfully, lovingly, poke her back. "I'm sorry. I'll call him later. Right now, I'm enjoying being with you."

Like So Many Pearls Before a Swine: A Love Story

Margot
Margaret
Marjorie
Margarida

part ~~one~~ ~~two~~ **three**

Margarethe
Margriet
Margisia
Marjatta

margot

The trip back was not as good as it could have been. Margot was a champ, though. She shrugged off her pain and hurt and tried to be pleasant for the few days it took us to get back home. In the hotel beds, she was receptive but not tender. I didn't bother her. I may be a swine, but I'm not a fucking swine.

I was really in my element on the trip back. We both were. The unwanted and unloved end of vacation outfits covered us like prison wear. No one imagines they will wear those extra things they pack, and normally we never do. We wouldn't be had it not been for getting caught in a sudden downpour as we were exploring a vineyard on the side of the highway. I even dropped Margot's camera, as I had predicted.

Huddled over a room service meal that last evening on the road, we were pensive but ready for a fight. Neither of us were for exploring the town we had decided to stop in before the last four-hundred-kilometre race home.

I drank timidly from a bottle of Vichy water while Margot taunted me with a vanilla Coke. We both picked at the salads but enormously enjoyed the Chicken Kiev despite ourselves.

"You're not drinking?"

"I can if you'd like."

She had rolled her eyes, spearing chicken on her fork and placing it in her mouth with a loud "Pff!"

The day of our return home is when I really shone, though. I really outdid myself on my little stage, posed in the kitchen, enjoying a slightly cooled bottle of Riesling as Margot walked in from unpacking her suitcase.

"I haven't put on the machine. I will if you've nothing to wash." Margot opens a bottle of water and pours herself a glass. She nods towards the glass in my hand. "How many glasses have you had? We haven't eaten yet."

"This is my second glass." The bottle sits on the counter, open, and reduced in volume by two glasses.

Margot walks over to the recycling bin and removes an empty Riesling bottle, holding it in front of her accusingly.

"Two glasses of *this* bottle, but in my defence, that one was almost empty." I stammer. Margot blinks at me and rather loudly returns the bottle to the bin.

"I don't have a problem, Margot." She had alluded to as much over her vanilla Coke the previous night.

"I never said you did."

"You said as much. Me or the wine. That's what you said."

"Because I want what I want. I know how you are before the bottle, and I know how you are after it. I choose before. So should you."

"What about me?"

Margot frowned at that, not unexpectedly. "What about you, *what*?"

"What do I get to demand?"

She closed her eyes. "This isn't *about* you. You do *know* that, right? This is about me and what I want. You claim to love me. So give me what I want. I don't think I'm being unfair."

"Ahh." I proudly answered like we were two lawyers jousting in a courtroom, and I had just found a chink in her legal armour.

"Look at me." Margot's voice, when necessary, is frighteningly strong. Not a little bit of adoration stems from fear, or perhaps you weren't aware of that. Fear is our attention and our focus. We fear what we are subject to, and we are very subject to what we love.

She repeated her words, but slower this time. "Look at me."

I looked at her. Boy, was she angry.

"You don't want to lose me. Not in the long term. You may think you do now, but that's just pride." She takes a mouthful of her water. "Little boy pride."

She leans back against the counter with folded arms, and I look at her, feeling bared and wretched. And then, out of nowhere, my tears come.

"No, you're right; I don't want to lose you. I don't want to hurt you either." I weep as she stands there looking at me. "But I keep on doing that."

"Hey." She reaches out, taking my hand. "Hey …"

After a while, I wipe my eyes and sniff. "I'm sorry." I laugh. "Just a scared little boy."

"What are you scared of?"

"You."

"That's silly."

"Is it?" I walk over to the table, take a Kleenex from the box and blow my nose. "It's not really, you know. I've been scared of you from the moment we first met. That's what adoration is, or love, or what you will. It's being under a spell and then offering yourself up and opening your heart. One is mesmerised and at the same time terrified."

"And do you know what?" Margot shakes her head, watching me. "At some point, you feel angry that your heart has been taken, angry that you are helpless in your adoration, so you poke holes in it, like a pin cushion., just to reassure yourself that you have some control of the situation."

I rub my face and look down longingly at the glass of wine sitting on the counter. "At least I do."

"Jesus." Margot exhales and turns to the glass cabinet. "Now I need a drink."

I laugh. "I'm sorry I'm such a bad influence, but I'll join you."

Things have been better since my outburst. Today, as I stand in the kitchen looking out over the garden, Margot returns from shopping, tosses her keys on the counter and places the small paper bag of victuals on the table. I have a glass of wine in my hand, which I have been inhaling and sipping over the last hour. Baby steps.

She feigns disinterest as she unpacks the bag. Cheese, unsalted nacho chips, organic tea. She reorganises the cupboard with her back to me, putting the new tea behind the old. She's very good about this and even puts washed plates beneath the others in the cabinet to rotate them. It makes sense. If you have six plates and only use two regularly, eventually, the other, bottom, four will never be used. Odd. I never thought about that until I met Margot.

She opens a package of cheese crackers, offering me one. I shake my head. "I told you. It's me or the wine."

I reach out. "Perhaps I will have one." She stretches out her arm so that I can reach the package. "You or wine. That's not really much of a choice."

She crunches and chews, folding up the foil and sliding it back into the cardboard box. She turns and places it in the cupboard. "Take it or leave it."

"I meant that as a compliment."

She turns back to me with an exasperated inhale of breath. "You're not on stage, you know. You needn't make everything you say or do charming."

"I know. Sorry." I smile, and not without a twinge of regret. pour the remaining wine in my glass into the sink. "I just wanted a last taste. That was an eighty-six Fumé Blanc too. I hope you're suitably impressed."

Margot raises her eyebrows. "Jesus. I thought you might have at least fought me for it."

I laugh. "Shall I? Honestly, I love you, and I want a life together. If I have to give up something for you, then so be it."

"Thank you." She smiles, nodding. "How about we meet in the middle. Wine with meals and just one glass a day." She closes the distance between us, and we kiss, holding each other.

"You know a bottle is six glasses. It may go bad."

She reaches up and presses her finger against my nose. "We'll buy half bottles."

margaret

We return after Annie, exhausted, panted her way over to where we sat talking about 'the guys back east', by way of our favourite vegan takeout for falafel and humus. This is food we usually make ourselves, but the long walk in the warm afternoon sun added to talk of my job offer has made us both tired and cautious. Food, ready to eat and packaged in bright-coloured paper, seemed to be the right thing to buoy our flagging mood.

"Is there Tzatziki?" Margaret peers into the carrying bag. "I'm in the mood for some. A lot."

I laugh. "How much is a lot?"

Margaret has already walked back to the open window and requested an extra container. "Do you have some small change?" She calls back.

I stuff my hands into the front pockets of my jeans, pull out a few coins, walk over and hand them to her. "Enough?"

"Perfect." She exchanges them for the treasured container of garlicky yoghurt, and smiling, places it in the bag with the rest of our food.

"Do we have Retsina at home?"

I laugh. "You really are in a specific mood."

She pouts. "No, it's just hot and I feel, I don't know. Your talk of moving made me think."

"Of wine?"

"No!" Margaret pushes against me playfully. "Of adventure, perhaps. I don't know. Besides. It's hot and I'm thirsty, and Retsina will go perfectly with all our stuff."

"I'm glad you decided on the whole round of bread too. Now we have the extra Tzatziki."

She nods. "Right? It's going to be yummy."

"Now *there's* a word I haven't heard you say … ever." I look at her as we walk back through the streets towards home. "The idea of moving. Has it made you curious?"

Margaret is silent for a moment, frowning slightly, playing with Annie's leash which she holds lightly but expertly in her hand.

"I think so. I mean, I can't move anywhere at the moment. But, at the end of the academic year? I could think of moving."

"Look, the wine store is still open." I point towards the small, corner, store with a slowly rotating inflatable wine bottle balloon waving about in front of the door. "I never thought that was a good idea."

Margaret laughs. "Because you're a wine snob." She hands me Annie's leash. "Wait here? I'll grab a bottle. Anything else?"

I shake my head. "Oh! Maybe they still have that Zweigelt we had last week."

She nods and enters the store. I can hear her voice greeting the owner. I love the sound of her voice. There's something cultured and smooth, learned and yet girlish about the sounds she makes when she talks. I can imagine it's a voice that would suit a singing career well. Come to think of it I don't think I've ever heard Margaret sing. A smoky jazz café. That's where her voice belongs. Nice.

I stand there lost in thought as my fantasy chanteuse serenades the heavy-lidded customers of some smoke-filled speakeasy, while the real Margaret is gently tugging the leash from my fingers.

"Hey. Sleepyhead. What's up?"

"Oh! Sorry. I was just thinking."

"That's something you do a lot, eh?" She begins walking away from me, Annie following at her side. "Think about how we're going to get into the apartment. I just realized I left my keys. Did you bring yours?"

"Hmm?" I blink twice, and then jog over to catch up. "Keys? No, I left them there. You were going to be at home, remember?"

Margaret exhales loudly. "I wonder if Mrs Fitch is home. She has our spare set."

"I've always wondered, why Mrs Fitch?"

"She's always home." Margaret laughs. "And, we don't have a garden to hide a set in."

I nod. "Hmm. Good point. We could leave a set on the balcony."

Margaret raises a sceptical eyebrow. "We're on the third floor, remember?"

I nod, quicker this time. "Riiight. Yes."

"Come on slowpokes, I'm getting thirsty. I want to get this wine in the freezer to quick chill."

Mrs Fitch is luckily at home.

We enjoy the takeout and the wine, then lay out on the balcony chairs, Annie resting peacefully beside us – but always quick to raise her head when a bird sings or a car honks on the street below.

The warm, summer air moves through the herbs and wildflowers that are arranged along the balcony railing pushing the green leaves and coloured petals this way and that in their pots.

Margaret's head lays next to mine, our fingers intertwined, gently moving and pressing against each other's for no other reason than a playful caress and the surety that we are there.

"The longer I think about it, the more I think you should take the job. I'm going to talk with the Dean on Monday." She turns her head to me and sits up slightly, her eyes staring into mine. "I can teach in New York."

"If you can make it there you can make it anywhere, right?" I smile, and run my fingers across her cheek, gently pressing her nose.

"Exactly." She lays back down. "I *can* make it anywhere."

"Of course, you can." We are both silent for a moment, reassured, taking this information and working it through our minds. Moving to another city. Together. "What about Annie?"

"What do you mean?"

"Big city. Much bigger city. City dogs. We'll need to find a place near a park."

"Central Park."

I laugh. "Yes, but not everyone lives around Central Park. I have no idea where I would live. It should be near the office."

"Where is the office?"

"I have honestly no idea. In New York?" I laugh. "I never thought about it. I wasn't intending to move there until a few minutes ago."

"Well, we can Google it."

"We can do that."

Margaret moves still closer to me. "Tell them you'll take the job. You can look for a nice flat for us when you're there."

"I love you."

"You better. I'd rather move to Seattle. Or Boston."

"Why Seattle or Boston?"

"I don't know. I don't have much connection to New York other than movies, media, the usual."

"What are your connections to Seattle or Boston?"

"Well, I was in Seattle quite a bit when I was younger."

"I never knew that."

"Hmm, and um, Boston. I don't know. I was there once. Oddly enough I saw the New York skyline on the way down the highway to Boston. I was at Brown University one summer. Anyway. I don't know. Boston always struck me as an interesting place. Maybe the public broadcasting channel. PBS. Well, and Harvard of course."

"Of course. Hm. Interesting."

"But I could do New York."

I lean over and kiss her. "I'm sure you could. Thank you."

"For what?"

"For us."

"Silly. Hey, look, if you dump me I'll still be in New York. Millions of guys."

I laugh. "Ahaha – the mercenary in you coming out loud and clear I see."

"The practical side of me."

"Is there any other side?"

"Hmm. No. No, I guess there isn't." She leans back over me and kisses me. "I love you."

"I know."

"Swine." She presses her lips strongly against mine, laughing. "Let's go Google where those guys back east lurk." She gets up and Annie immediately rises. "Come on Annie – let's go see if we can find you some nice big city parks."

Annie barks, I get up, and the three of us walk inside.

marjorie

"Why haven't we ever gotten married?"

Marjorie looks at me with large, almond eyes, from above her spongecake slice, half in, half out of her mouth.

I lean over and brush a few errant crumbs from her sweater. "Is it because I've waited too long to ask? I was meaning to." I get this in before she has the chance to respond. You may think me cruel mentioning this, but she did say she didn't want any dessert.

The spongecake is a spur of the moment purchase from the buffet cart as it made its way noisily down the aisle shortly after the train's failed departure. Twenty minutes ago, and hardly five metres down the track, the train came to a sudden stop.

"Oh no. I hope we aren't going to be here long. Do you know, I think I *will* have something sweet."

"You have me?"

Marjorie had rolled her eyes and waved to the steward. "Forgive me if I don't bite into you just at the moment."

Majorie coughs slightly, and I pass her an opened bottle of water, a bit worried she'll choke. My timing has never been good.

She takes a sip and swallows, then coughs again, breathing in deeply, following that up with a glare in my direction.

"Are you completely insane?"

"Only when I look at you. Your beauty …"

Marjorie widens her eyes and leans forward. This I know from past experience is her way of asking 'do you know how close to death you are right now'?

I lift my hands in front of me to ward off any blows. "I'm sorry. Bad timing. I was thinking of asking and then asked before I saw you had your mouth full." I take her hands, which she tries to pull away. I smile, not melting her but she hasn't taken her hands back so I'm safe to continue.

"I *am* sorry." I release her hands.

Marjorie wipes her mouth with the napkin on her lap. "You're a complete beast. I was enjoying that cake."

"I'm *very* sorry."

"I think you meant to do that."

"Honestly not. No."

"Well, if you want an answer, then I'll give you one. We've never married because you're a beast."

"I am. I'm sorry."

She sits back and breathes in and out for a few minutes. Then, she sits back up and looks at me. "What sort of question *is* that anyway?"

"I don't know. I was wondering. We've been together for a lot of years. We've never talked about it. Have we?"

Marjorie rolls her eyes. "Maybe I'll just move to another seat."

"No! No. sorry." I laugh, which makes things *so* much better.

Marjorie begins to rise. "Yes, moving sounds good."

"Oh, wait! Haha, look I'm really sorry. It just sort of came out. Darling. Please."

Marjorie sits down. I don't know if she's angry or just playing. At any rate, I gently hold her hands and look at her. "I'm serious. I was just thinking. It's been such a nice day together. Until now. Heh heh, but that's my fault. It just sort of popped out. I mean, we're together most of the time, I love you, I hope you love me. I was just … wondering."

"You love me? Awww that's sweet. Poorly timed, but sweet."

"Of course I love you. Didn't you know that?"

"Honestly?"

"No, lie to me. I like that." I smile.

"You're the worst. Really. Honestly, I don't think you've ever said you love me."

"Oh."

"Yes. You're horrible."

"I just assumed you knew."

"Did you send me a text? You know, something along the lines of you loved me? Perhaps I never received it. Was it in an email? You do know how these things get lost. All the time as a matter of fact."

"Okay, okay, you're right. I should take this more seriously."

"You should if you want to marry me."

"So there's hope! I mean … I mean you'd consider it?"

"At this rate, maybe not. You've got a lot of ground to back pedal, fella."

"But it sounded like there was hope."

Majorie laughs. "There's always hope. Even for you." She leans over and kisses me. "I know you love me. Don't worry."

"This is awkward."

"Agreed. Tell me about your meeting with Peter."

"Right! I never did."

"You never asked me about my shopping either."

"We were occupied finding a taxi."

"And eating. And you spent a lot of time watching me."

"I do that a lot, don't I? Though, if I can be honest, I really like looking at you. You're beautiful. I could just watch you go about your day and be perfectly happy."

"You *are* a nut."

"So. What did you buy anyway? I probably didn't ask because you didn't have any shopping bags when we met. You don't, do you?"

Marjorie shakes her head. "No. I didn't find anything I wanted."

"I'm sorry."

"Bad luck. Next time perhaps. It was nice walking around though. Now. Tell me about your meeting."

"To tell the truth it was a long way to come for a coffee. It was a duty call. I don't think anything will come of it, but I needed to make an appearance if I want any work from him."

"Do you think that's going to happen?"

Now it's my turn to shake my head. "Probably not."

I sit back and we both let out a sigh.

"I don't think either of us will remember this trip as being our most successful."

"You said you loved me."

"True. And you hinted that we may even get married. *And* I made a few good social media posts as well. So, not a total loss then."

Marjorie slaps my hand and then keeps hers on top of mine. Her soft, warm fingers envelop mine.

I turn my head and look at her smiling face. "It won't make any difference to me, getting married or not. I'm quite content with how things are. There's only you in my life. I'm happy."

"There's the tax benefits."

"Oh. I'd forgotten about those. Then how come you didn't ask me years ago? We could have saved a fortune!"

"You're joking, right?"

"You're gullible."

"You're beautiful."

"You said that already."

"You're right." I smile, the train finally jerks to a start, and we move clumsily forward out of the station.

margarida

The not so gentle meowing of Margarida's three cats wake me before the alarm. The sun is almost up, but the girls want some attention.

"Mmm, I'll get them." Margarida's voice, thick with sleep, slurs from beneath the pillow beside me.

"It's okay. You sleep. I'll take care of it."

I get up, careful not to step on any of the feline mistresses of the house, and walk into the hallway. The girls follow.

"Good morning ladies. Are you hungry? Or would you like something else?"

The dry cat food is still relatively full. I take up the wet food dish, scrub it out under the tap, and fill it with Gourmet Grilled Seafood. Obviously, packaging like this is meant more for the purchaser than the animal eating it. I take a quick glance at the back of the package. "It says here it's a carefully sourced balance of fine seafood and sauce." I look down at one of the cats now eagerly eating. "I wonder what they mean by carefully sourced?"

The other girls are eager for the water coming out of the spout, so I turn that to cold and reduce the volume. "Does anyone want to go outside?" I open the window leading to the balcony so anyone wishing to jump out for a morning stretch can do so.

Then I fill the kettle and plug it in. I look at the clock. Six fifteen. The alarm will go off shortly. I take two cups from the cupboard and place a Darjeeling teabag in each, then I go back into the bedroom and slip beneath the covers.

Margarida is warm and aromatic, lovely to press against and enjoy. I could stay like this for a while.

"Are you inhaling me?"

"Not really."

"What are you doing then? I can hear you."

"I'm insufflating you."

"Haha – nice. Well, leave some of me, please. I have a lot to do today."

I kiss her cheek. "I promise I won't breathe all of you in."

"Thank you." She turns and returns my kiss. "Good morning. Thanks for taking care of the girls."

"My pleasure. I'm making tea."

"Mm, you're sweet."

"Want to have a shower first? I'm not in a rush."

"I will, yes. I need to drive over and get more clay."

"Do you need some help?"

"That would be nice, but on the way, I need to run a few other errands, so I'll be gone for a while. The vet for one."

"Okay. Well, let me know if I can help. Then, I'll make the tea and bring you in a cup."

"I'll leave most of the clay in the car. You can help me bring that up later if you like. It's heavy."

I nod, we kiss, part, and as I fetch the cups of tea, the bathroom radio turns on and cool jazz resonates out from the half-open bathroom door.

"Here you are. I'll leave it on the windowsill. Want me to open the window?"

"Please. Thanks for the tea."

"Do you need any help in there?" I playfully tease.

"Haha, you know, I think I'll be fine. You did so much already last night."

"Ah, you're so kind. I did, didn't I?"

"Heh heh, braggart."

I leave the bathroom, walk into the living room and out onto the balcony to enjoy the early morning sunshine.

A short scream from inside brings me back into the living room. "Margarida? What was that?" I walk quickly down the hallway into the bathroom. Margarida is laying on the floor, crying.

"Oh my God. What happened?" I kneel, covering her with a bath towel.

"I slipped. I reached for the towel, my foot moved one way, then I moved the other. Oh damn! I think I've done something to my knee."

"Can you try and stand?"

Margarida pushes herself up with my assistance, but putting weight on her right leg causes her pain. "Sit here, next to the bathtub." I look at her leg. "You had problems with your knee before, haven't you?" She nods. "Let's get dressed and I'll take you to the Emergency."

"Oh no. I don't have time for that. I've got so much to do. Damn!"

We sit in silence for some time, I pass her the cup of tea, and the girls come and go, staring at us for a while, then wandering away again.

"Why don't I help you into the bedroom. We can wrap your knee, keep it up, see how it is later. Umm ... I can run your errands."

"You've got things to do today as well."

"I can postpone them. No teaching today. All postponable."

"Could you?"

"I could. I will."

"Thank you."

I smile. "Look, let's get you dried off and dressed. Then we'll see how you're doing when I get back. I'll need a list?"

Margarida nods. "Okay. Yes."

With Margarida resting in the bedroom making up a list of tasks for me to handle, I get onto my own calls and postpone the day's activities.

"All ready?" I return to the bedroom and sit on the bed next to her. "What can I bring before I go?"

"Water? Something to eat? My phone too, please. Thank you."

I return with a bottle of mineral water, a package of hobnobs, and Margarida's phone. "Anything else?"

She looks at me with tears in her eyes. "Oh no. You know, if I can't move my knee I can't use my wheel!" Margarida begins to cry. I put the items on the bedside table and take her in my arms. "I can't believe this. What horrible timing."

Margarida's potter's wheel was given to her by her mother. A beautiful, wooden kick wheel, made before the electric wheels came into common use.

"What shall I do?"

I'm a bad doctor, but an even worse potter. In fact, I can't throw a ball of clay to save my life.

"Look. Rest. I'll run the errands, and we'll talk when I come back." I lean over and kiss her. "I love you."

Margarida sniffs and wipes away her tears. "Thank you. I love you too."

"Call me if you need anything, okay?" She nods, and I walk out of the bedroom, and out of the apartment.

While waiting for the clay to be loaded into the trunk of my car it occurs to me that an electric potter's wheel might save the day. "A thousand dollars, and delivered tomorrow?"

The clerk nods. "That's right. I'm sorry to hear about Margarida. We'll deliver it free of charge. She was really excited about getting that project with the library."

"She is. Now she's afraid she won't be able to see it through. Thank you. It's very kind."

The clerk smiles. "It's my pleasure. Margarida is a pearl."

"She is." I nod my head, pocketing the receipt. "I couldn't have said it any better myself."

margarethe

Friday night arrives surprisingly quickly. I say surprisingly because I find any time I'm looking forward to something it seems to take a horribly long time to arrive. Birthdays, Christmas, vacation, the proof of your next book … some of these things take ages. It gets easier with age because we're so busy. It's probably worse for kids.

We don't live together so I always look forward to seeing Margarethe. As we don't spend too many nights together, I feel always on tenterhooks, even at my advanced age. I always seem to be in a state of extreme desire.

How many *too many* might be I'm not sure. And is sex once every other week enough? Is it once a week? Not living together, it doesn't seem like many nights nor enough sex. However, it's probably on average the norm.

I read an article that said couples had sex on average two to three times a month, which doesn't seem like much at all. I wonder who they asked?

I thought as I got older I would put desire behind me, but it's simply not happened. I think about sex just as much at sixty as I did at sixteen.

Hanging very far out on a wobbly limb I'm going to suggest that the male sex drive is stronger and lasts later in life than the female – purely from a biological consideration.

I stare long and hard at myself in the mirror. If Margarethe wasn't sensitive to the aroma of cologne I would splash some on. I'm feeling daring. Also if I owned any cologne. After we started dating I got rid of the few bottles I had.

How long am I going to stand here looking at myself? I look at my watch. It had better not be for much longer.

Forty minutes later I ring Margarethe's doorbell and she buzzes me in.

"Hey." Her head peeps out from the half-open door.

"Hi." I walk in and she shuts the door behind me. "Sorry, I'm late."

She takes my jacket. "Are you late?"

"I feel like I'm late."

She looks at her watch. "You're right on time."

"Oh." We embrace, and then kiss. "That's all right then."

She frowns and tilts her head. "Are you all right?" Laughing, she walks down the hallway in the direction of the kitchen.

"Fine." I laugh and follow her.

Once in the kitchen, she motions me to my usual chair at the end of the wooden table. "Would you like something to drink?"

"Please. Whatever you're having. Wine?"

Margarethe nods. "Red?"

"Perfect."

She pours me a glass from the almost empty bottle of Chianti standing on the table. "Thank you. Is this the bottle from our last dinner?"

"Yes. You'll need to open another bottle please." She looks at me, smiles, and returns to the chopping block on the counter on which she is grating parmesan cheese.

"Actually." I drink from my glass. A glass of courage they call it. "There was something I wanted to talk with you about."

She laughs and turns to me. "I thought you seemed odd."

"There's nothing wrong. It can wait until after dinner."

Margarethe walks towards me, wiping her hands on her apron. "No, let's talk about whatever is bothering you now. I'll be thinking about it all through dinner otherwise."

I smile. "It's really okay. After dinner is fine."

She gives me her sternest expression. "Please just tell me now. I insist."

"You insist?"

"Yes."

I clear my throat and take another mouthful of courage, before getting up from the chair which creaks in gratitude as my weight removes itself. I then get down on one knee as Margarethe's hands go up to her face, bring the open box with the ring up in my hand, and ask her. "Margarethe, I love you. Will you marry me?"

"What did you say?" Margarethe stops her cutting board ministrations and turns.

"Hmm?" I look up, back from my daydream. "Oh! Sorry, nothing. I was just talking to myself."

"Ah. Well, why don't you talk to me? I've been thinking about you all day."

I stand up and walk over to her, nuzzling her neck and kissing her cheek. "Careful, or we'll be having my fingers for dinner."

"Mmm, I wouldn't mind having you for dinner."

Margarethe nudges me away. "Go. Open the wine and tell me about your day. Mine was a complete clutter fuck."

I take up the bottle of wine, cut the cap off with the small knife at the side of the corkscrew, and then push the screw into the cork. "Cluster fuck. The expression you're looking for, Darling."

"Oh. Yes! Yes, that was it. I knew it was something like that."

I laugh. "You're adorable."

"I know. You remind me daily."

"Mea Culpa."

"No, no. Praise on Helicanus, praise on."

"What?"

Margarethe laughs. "So. Something you don't know. Helicanus. The loyal servant of Pericles? Shakespeare? The bard?"

"Hahaha, yes, I've heard of Shakespeare thank you, m'lady."

We both laugh and I remove the cork from the bottle. "Would you like a glass?"

Margarethe nods her head. "Please."

"So. Why was your day so bad?"

"Oh, you know. The usual. People weren't prepared, they went off-topic at the first chance during the project meeting, any agenda deteriorated into chaos. Your typical day. How was yours?"

I chuckle. "In comparison, surprisingly untypical."

"You got a lot done?"

"I did."

Margarethe wipes her hands on her apron, tosses her handiwork into a hot frying pan and, satisfied with the sizzling sounds in front of her smiles. "Okay. I think we'll be eating soon."

"What's on the menu?" I peer into the pan, and at the pot of simmering something on the back burner.

"It's a surprise."

I frown. "A good surprise or a bad surprise?" I venture, receiving a smack on my arm for my curiosity.

"Here." Margarethe hands me napkins and cutlery stacked on top of two large plates. "Please do the honours."

I put my glass down on the counter and set the table.

"It smells good. Whatever it is you're surprising me with."

"Good." She smiles in return. "It's something new I'm trying."

Always dangerous to comment on, I think to myself.

"I like what you usually make."

"Well, then I may make this again. Then you'll like it too."

I smile. "I love you. Have I told you that lately?"

"I'm sure you have." She kisses me as she passes. "I love you too."

Dinner is, of course, delicious, and after dinner, Margarethe asks me to marry her.

margriet

A month after moving into our first, and last flat, three cardboard boxes remain in the hallway unpacked and seemingly unloved. Did you have a box or two like this when you last moved?

In the first months of preparing to up stakes, items are slowly and lovingly sorted, wrapped, labelled with care and itemized on the mover's inventory sheets. As the days draw closer to the actual date of the move, however, boxes are folded into shape and the most random of last-minute items are loaded in. the items we didn't bring ourselves to throw away, but also perhaps the items we couldn't do without.

My briefcase, upon opening, revealed a virtual treasure chest of trinkets that in my last flat occupied my desk drawer, and then my tabletop, the kitchen counter, and finally found their way into the last ship leaving port, my briefcase.

Margriet and I often ventured to open the boxes now sitting in the hallway. We would peek in and peruse their contents. Pick something up – the lucky items actually making their way into a drawer or another box – safe but still in a sort of limbo.

Eventually, these boxes will move to the storage room, and will probably never see the light of day. The orphans of the move.

I look around my bedroom office, or is it my office bedroom? Possibly it's my office room. At any rate, the room in which I work and very often sleep. It has not been a good first month.

"I've decided I would prefer a bedroom and an office." I've knocked on Margriet's bedroom office or office bedroom, and after a moment she stops typing and looks up over the rims of her glasses. I love it when she does that, but this is not the moment for me to adore her.

She looks back down and types to the end of her thought then looks up again. "I thought you wanted your peace."

"I miss you."

"I'm right here."

"I'm sorry."

She removes her glasses and rubs her tired eyes. "I'm sorry too. Why are you so complicated? You're like a little boy."

"I know."

"Why do you make it so difficult for me to love you?"

"I don't know."

She replaces her glasses and returns to her work. After a few minutes she still has not looked up at me, which I take as a sign that she has no more to say, so I retreat to the kitchen. There I pour myself a large glass of scotch, taking this to the living room.

Halfway through my glass, and an equal distance through my book, Margriet comes into the living room and sits on the arm of the sofa, running her hands over the pale blue material.

"I love this sofa."

"So do I."

"I'm going to go away for the weekend, to see Beth. Remember I told you?"

I nod.

"When I return, I'd like you to have decided what you want regarding the bedroom and office. Okay?"

I nod again.

She smiles weakly, stands up and walks back out of the room.

I'm really such an idiot.

The next day I drive Margriet to the station with her small, black, overnight bag.

"Don't watch pornography all weekend, Dear."

"But …"

She smiles and leans over to kiss me. "I'm joking. I love you; you know that I hope?"

"I do."

She smiles, painfully almost, turns, and walks towards the platform, losing herself in the crowds of people crisscrossing the station's busy concrete stage.

I am better than my word, springing into action upon my return from the station and before the car's engine has even fully cooled.

Into the storage room go the orphaned boxes. Dismantled and equally relegated downstairs goes my bed, the sheets hitting the laundry and the non-washables the fresh air on our long balcony. I vacuum like a madman, though there is very little dust it is more of a ceremonial act.

Moving my desk, and that of Margriet is much more of an ordeal, and I am glad of the extra day available so that I can carefully first photograph her desktop and then transport the desk and things into the office, making sure everything is as she left it albeit it another room.

The next morning I fill the free space now obvious in the bedroom with a plinth from the living room on top of which sit one each of our early artistic attempts at sculpture. However, upon consideration after many walks in and out of the bedroom, the art fails to be convincing.

Using the opportunity to walk to the market, I stock up on items for dinner and replace the artworks with a vase of vibrant yellow tulips. Much better.

I find two pieces of paper and write bedroom on one, and office on the other, as we had on moving day, and tape them to their respective door frames.

I look at my watch and rub the bristles on my jaw. It's almost time to pick Margriet up from the station. I look at my reflection in the hall mirror. Throwing all caution to the wind I undo the top button of my shirt, and, after deciding not to shave, I leave the flat and drive to the station.

Ninety minutes later I'm pretty sure I've either mistaken the time of her arrival or possibly the platform when I receive a text.

What did you do to the flat???

What are you doing at home? I'm here at the station.

What are you doing at the station?

Surprising you!

You did that. You moved my desk. Where is the day bed?

Gone

Oh. Are you coming back?

I can. Should I? Are you mad?

Why? What else have you done??

I mean, a sane person would just have called.

I stop by the bakery on my way home, picking up a small selection of sticky buns, some of which I know are Margriet's favourite. Upon arrival, I find her ensconced in the kitchen enjoying a sticky bun with a cup of coffee.

"Oh! You stopped by the bakery as well." I hold my bag aloft.

She smiles. "Yes. I'm sorry. I brought you something too."

I walk to the counter and peer into a bag, the twin of that which I hold. "Mmm raisin brioche. Thank you."

I walk over and kiss Margriet on the cheek. "Welcome home. I hope this wasn't too shocking."

She returns my kiss, then turns her attention to the remains of her bun. "It wasn't a bad shock. You were busy. My desk looks identical to when I left it. That was interesting to see." She smiles.

"I took pictures before moving it."

Margriet laughs. "You're such a nut." She stands up and walks to the coffee machine. "I'll make you a coffee."

"Thank you." I place the second bag of buns on the counter. "How was your trip? How's Beth?"

"It was nice. A bit stressful. You know how trains can be. We had a nice time." Margriet hands me a cup, warm to the touch, filled with coffee and steamed milk.

"Mm, thank you."

"And what did you get up to? Besides the interior redecorating?"

"Mostly watched porn. I was so tempted when you told me not to." I laugh, removing a brioche from the bag and biting into it. "Mm, these are good. Still warm."

Margriet laughs. "Beth and I did the same thing. It was like being in college again."

I stop chewing, imagining the scene. "Really?" I mew, my mouth half full of brioche and surprise.

"Hahaha, you're such a pig." Margriet laughs. "I'm pulling your leg. But it's interesting that you believed me."

I shake my head. "I didn't." I'm able to express my indignation now, the brioche successfully chewed and swallowed. "I was just playing along."

Margriet winks. "I know. However, as you've made the bedroom so pretty and there are no work distractions, perhaps we can climb into bed and …"

She smiles seductively and walks out of the kitchen and I quickly follow.

margisia

The museum and the walk in the park are wonderful. I felt guilty most of the early afternoon as we wandered about with nothing other to do than hold hands and look at things. But I am back in my comfort zone after an early dinner of salad and bread, watching Margisia shuffling cards in the kitchen.

"May I deal?"

She looks up and cuts the cards twice, then slides them across to me. "Don't deal me garbage, okay?"

I smile and begin slowly dealing the cards. "I promise."

"Don't you want to try some other games?"

"What did you have in mind?"

"I don't know. Chess?"

"Chess?" She frowns and looks at her cards, sorting them as she picks them up.

"Sure, why not?"

"You'd have to teach me."

"I can do that."

"Let me think about it."

We play our hands silently for the next few minutes, Margisia beating me easily.

I let out a playful sigh. "You're slaughtering me."

She reaches over and takes my hand. "I'm sorry." She smiles. "Do you know what we could do? We could walk down to the river. There's a concert tonight." She looks at her watch. "It starts in an hour. We'd easily make it."

"You know it's a school night, right?"

Margisia laughs. "A school night? I haven't heard that since I was a girl."

"No, I mean we both have to leave early in the morning to teach. Do you need to do any prep beforehand?"

She shakes her head. "It's just revision tomorrow. How about you?"

I shake my head. "Same. Well, mostly revision. I like springing things on them when they're least expecting it."

Margisia laughs. "You're so cruel."

"Well, they're not going to be warned about everything that comes at them in life. They need to prepare for the unexpected."

"I thought you were teaching an online marketing course? It sounds more like you're training assault troops."

I laugh. "Online marketing *requires* assault troops." I walk into the hallway, looking for my wallet. "Do we need money?"

"Perhaps. Could you bring some? I didn't get to the bank today."

"Sure. If I can find my wallet."

"It's probably in your laptop bag."

I open my bag and sure enough, there is my wallet. "Got it."

Margisia comes into the hallway from the bedroom, her long hair tied at the back of her neck by a thick, red scarf.

"That looks nice."

"What?" She looks at herself in the mirror and then takes her jacket from the rack.

"Your scarf. It looks nice. You look nice."

She smiles. "You're always far too kind about my appearance."

"It will be my undoing." I take my own jacket from the hanger and slip it on.

Margisia comes up to me, kissing me quickly with her soft, red lips. "What a way to go."

"Exactly!" I laugh as we leave the apartment, locking the door behind us.

The park is home to two bandstands, and we're fortunate that the concert is being held at the smaller one which is closest. After about thirty minutes, we reach the space by way of her street, the woods, and a walk along the river. The night is still warm, but fresh, and it being a weekday evening the venue is not too crowded. Actually, a pleasant way to spend the evening.

"This was a good idea."

"Wasn't it?"

I nod. "Yes."

"What would you do without me?"

"Win at cards?" I laugh, and she pokes me in the ribs.

"You can't win at everything. Losing at cards is a small price to pay for having won me."

"Hmm. I never thought about it that way before." I take her hand as we walk towards the small crowd of people standing about the bandstand. Musicians are warming up, filling the air with a mild cacophony of horns and strings. "So, if I won you, what am I to you? Considering my poor card skills."

Margisia squeezes my hand and giggles. "You're my booby prize." She teases. "Shh! She hushes my attempted protest with a finger pressed gently against my lips. "The music is starting."

We stand there for forty-five minutes listening to the music, pressed against each other, Margisia in the front, me with my arms wrapped around her from behind, alternatingly leaning against and supporting the other throughout the performance.

There isn't much you can do during a concert. You can watch the musicians, listen to the music, look about. There's little to comment on. You are, in fact, looking at the source of the music. People used to look at the radio when it was the boxy centrepiece one day to be replaced by television. We used to look at stereos too.

It's funny that people dress up to sit and watch an orchestra play too. What are we looking at, and why are we dressed up? Rock concerts are the worst. You need a pair of binoculars to see the tiny people performing on the stage in the distance. Unless you are near the stage, which always seems like an extremely dangerous place to be. Watching musicians. Odd when you think about it. At least with dance and opera, there is some movement on stage. Something to see.

You can talk during a concert, of course, but we never said a word. I had the feeling our thoughts were following each other anyway. We seemed to know when the other wanted to shift weight when the music called for a tighter or a stronger hold, and when a kiss was called for.

As we walk back the sun is dipping down towards the horizon, and we're happy we brought jackets.

"It cooled down quickly."

"Yes. It was nice though, right?"

"Really nice. Thanks for suggesting it."

We take each other's hands and walk back the way we had come, slower this time, not needing to be anywhere other than exactly where we were.

"Was that better than losing at cards?"

I laugh. "Immensely better."

"Maybe you can teach me chess then. We can mix it up a bit. I don't want you to be unhappy."

"Thank you. I'm not unhappy, and I don't mind losing."

"I don't want you to get bored."

"I won't. I have you. And that's really all I want. You can beat me at cards or at chess, which you probably will eventually." I laugh. "I just want to be with you."

Margisia squeezes my hand, and I look over to her as she smiles. "Come on. Let's get back and into bed."

"Mm, yes. Another great suggestion." I nod, and without another word, our pace quickens, out of the woods and up the hill towards home.

marjatta

"What are you thinking?"

What do I say to that? What can I say? I'm thinking about the days when Marjatta and I first met, the night we first kissed, the night she invited me into her bed, the days and weeks when we weren't talking to each other, the months when we went about our lives, each day together.

I'm thinking about my life before the day we met, about some of the wasted time when we were apart, and how fast time flew when we were together.

I'm thinking about what would have been, had other things not gotten in the way. Oh and everything else on top. My childhood and how bad a father I was and all the stupid things I did, as I guess we all did when we were younger. Life really is incredibly ridiculous in retrospect. Most of the time you have to laugh. Or cry.

"Why are you laughing?" Marjatta looks up at me.

"Sorry. I was just thinking to myself."

"About?"

We've returned to our favourite town on the water. To our favourite café and hotel. To familiar places, we can enjoy without any stress of the unknown. We have returned for one last holiday.

We're sitting together on a long wooden bench someone placed on the dike between the footbridge in the north and a bicycle bridge in the south. It's about a kilometre from end to end, so the bench is perfect for us. What is the difference between a bicycle bridge and a footbridge? Well, other than the speed of crossing, wooden slats of the footbridge are laid lengthwise, and those making up the bicycle bridge are laid widthwise. Someone in the park's planning department was on the ball that day.

Marjatta nudges me. "Hmm?" I turn to her as she takes my arm in her hands, gripping gently but firmly for my attention.

She could always pull what she wanted from me. She just had to tug at me with her beautiful, almond eyes, her small yet strong hands. Marjatta has a built-in insistence which is adorable if you are only hiding a very small secret.

Of course, the doctor had told her the results, just as I had expected him to but she made me own up anyway. And Marjatta scolded me anyway which was the least I deserved. She shut herself in her room for a day and kept the door locked so my heart fractured a little more than the lab results said it already was. Fissures lengthening with each passing minute. I had to suffer alone when I heard her crying through the night. That was the beginning of my punishment and I guess I deserved it.

Over the next few days, she made calls and left me notes and directions, papers to sign and tasks to complete. If I wasn't going to fight, then I had to sit on the sidelines was her message. This was all going to be on her and was good practice if she was going to be left alone. Again. At the end of the week, it was my turn to weep my heart out, and she left me to do that alone too, to complete my penance.

"You know it won't make any difference. I'm not going to suffer just to stay alive. I'm also not going to let you nurse me. I always told you that. You rip off a plaster quickly, Marjatta. It hurts like hell, but it hurts worse if you pull it off bit by bit over time."

"Why do you get to decide that?"

"I didn't decide. This was decided for both of us."

Dr Yates stopped by after a few days and took my side, but you could see he wanted to take Marjatta's. Six months isn't a very long time, but we would make the most of it. Marjatta was a strong woman. She would be fine. Honestly, I felt that it was me suffering more, knowing there would be days and nights and weeks and probably years where I would not be here with her. This hurt more than anything that was happening to my body.

"I wondered what you were thinking about. You're so quiet. Except for the sudden hiccups of laughter. Quite odd." She smiles.

I laugh and look at her. "I was thinking about things."

She turns and looks out across the wind-driven water, pointing out a heron that has just landed.

"I was recalling, when I was younger, how I feared dying. I never liked the idea."

She laughs. "I don't think many people do."

I chuckle. "Agreed."

"You still don't. I know. I'm sorry. I wish I could do something."

I squeeze her hand in mine. "I know. I love you, and I'm sorry that I'm leaving again. I always seem to be leaving you."

In the distance, the lighthouse on the coast starts up its beacon, slowly churning the darkening sky with its strong, yellow, light.

"I always want to know what's going to happen at the end of a story, and when I like the story enough, I never want it to end."

Marjatta nods. We've talked about this before. I'm insufferable when I finish a book, or we've watched the final episode of an excellent television series. Once I make that sort of connection, it's very hard for me to end it.

"I've been thinking lately that I'm fine now because I know how the story is going to end, and even though I'd like it to go on, I'm happy with it." Marjatta looks at me. "I'm happy that it's ending with you. That we're together. I can't think of any other ending to my life that would be as perfect."

Marjatta leans her head against my shoulder. "Ah, you … you're making me cry, and the wind is blowing."

I laugh and place my hand on her cheek, covering her eyes from the cold. "I'm sorry. Bad timing. Shall we go?"

"No. Let's stay here together a while longer and watch the sunset."

We sit on the long wooden bench, together reliving memories of all those perfect moments we've shared as the sun slowly makes its way towards the horizon. Marjatta's fingers rub the pearls of her necklace, her head moving closer to my chest for warmth. The quiet evening is broken only by the hum of our voices and, at times, the odd snort of my laughter.

Printed in Great Britain
by Amazon